THE ALIEN

They had put Ed Landini, the gravely injured astronaut, into a "poster" terminal for instant transmission to an Earth hospital.

What arrived was . . . a biped of vaguely canine appearance in an unfamiliar type of spacesuit. Somehow the "poster" had achieved contact with a being from an alien universe!

When the creature recovered consciousness, it spoke in English—and told a nurse a dirty joke.

When they asked the alien its name, it said, "Ed Landini—of course."

Also by John Brunner
Published by Ballantine Books:

THE SHEEP LOOK UP

THE WHOLE MAN

THE SQUARES OF THE CITY

THE SHOCKWAVE RIDER

STAND ON ZANZIBAR

DOUBLE, DOUBLE

THE INFINITIVE OF GO

John Brunner

A Del Rey Book

BALLANTINE BOOKS • NEW YORK

A Del Rey Book
Published by Ballantine Books

Library of Congress Catalog Card Number: 79-90155

ISBN 0-345-28497-6

Manufactured in the United States of America

First Edition: February 1980

Cover art by Darrell K. Sweet

ONE

*to travel faster
than a speeding bullet
is not much help
if you and it
are heading straight
towards each other*

"I'd be much happier," grumbled the ambassador, "if I understood how these damned posters work."

In a formal high-necked jacket and dark pants he, and his companion the first secretary who was almost identically clad, looked like intruders in the deep-dug concrete-lined redoubt concealed beneath the embassy. Everybody else present wore color-coded oversuits, even the man who, posing as a trade counselor, was responsible for gathering and forwarding local intelligence data.

Because nations are never friendly in the paranoid universe inhabited by spies, the latter would normally have been in command of any operation of this sort. But the current one was devoid of precedent. A specially-trained technician had been flown in under cover of forged documents and an improvised trade agreement. So far as this room at present was concerned he outranked everybody, although his oversuit was indistinguishable except by its tint from those worn by the lowly Marine guards standing bored beside the armored door.

It was not his first visit; he had set up an earlier, smaller installation when its parts—like the new one's—

were delivered by devious means. Not looking up from the dials, gauges and meters which were engaging his attention, he said now, "With respect, Mr. Ambassador, the fewer people who do understand it, the better for us all."

"Yes. Yes, of course," sighed the ambassador, and went on staring at the poster.

It was a nondescript-looking cabinet about the size of two telephone booths side by side, which occupied the center of the floor and reached nearly to the low, two-meter-twenty ceiling. Its front was a transparent door; its walls might at a glance have been taken for blocks of the kind of solid plastic used for mass-produced disposable articles a generation earlier, when there was still cheap oil.

In fact those drab brown walls were dense with microcircuitry. Every cubic millimeter of them, and the floor and roof as well, contained a maze of sensors and logic units, some mere molecules wide. It had taken nearly as long to grow them, under controlled conditions, as the nervous system of a moderately advanced mammal: a dog or a horse.

Yet it was already one of dozens such, and there were hundreds more in preparation, and into the bargain there was only a quantitative, not a qualitative difference between these circuits and the ones which, built into the embassy's walls, had for the past decade ensured its immunity from bugging, eavesdropping and even sniping.

All of which advance in security did not prevent the ambassador from saying fretfully, "Even so, I keep wondering whether a bomb might arrive when you switch the thing on . . ."

The first secretary raised an eyebrow at the trade counsellor, and he favored her with a broad grin behind the ambassador's back. The technician finished his checks and set aside his testing instruments.

Patiently he said, "There is literally no way that

could happen. Not even if someone stole the programs from the dozen or fifteen different factories where the various parts are made. We have enough trouble matching two units that we've built ourselves. For someone trying to imitate one from scratch, it would be a nightmare." He consulted a clock on the wall which was governed by a master-signal relayed via satellite from half the world away. It showed that more than a minute remained before the intended time of transfer.

"I have to take your word," sighed the ambassador. "But you must forgive me for being on edge. After all, a live human is very different from a mere—well—package!"

"We never had any trouble with non-living consignments," the first secretary countered.

"There was one group so badly garbled—" began the trade counselor; she cut him short.

"One group out of how many hundreds? Given that most of us can't even make a phone-call home from this damnable country, diplomatic priority or no, I think you ought to count yourself fortunate in having so much cipher-traffic!"

The first secretary's complaints about how her tour here was apt to ruin her marriage were public knowledge. The counselor said placatingly, "Oh, I'm alive to the fact that this is a wonderful invention. The small version has brought in more information faster and by a more secure route than ever before, and we have a head start with the technique over everyone else on the planet. Aren't I right?"

The technician gave a wry smile.

"The Japanese have comparable computing capacity, remember, so in principle they might be on to it. If they were, how the hell could we find out? But myself, I do believe the States have a clear lead. What we have here is almost unique—an invention that has genuinely been kept secret even after it went into regular operation. And pretty soon it won't just be information that we're posting, but weaponry, H-bombs, armies!" He pointed at the clock. "Coming up to zero now," he added. "Quiet, please!"

They all fell silent. They had seen objects arrive by poster before; they were prepared for the curious wash of pale violet light which would announce a delivery to the interior of the cabinet. But the ambassador was right. The transmission of a live human being was a new benchmark in this new technology, even though back home there had been plenty of tests on volunteers and no ill-effects had been detected.

The clock ticked away the last few seconds, and there was the violet flash, and there *he* was, known to them, recognizable: a man of thirty-five or so, about one meter eighty tall, slim, fair-haired, grey-eyed, wearing unremarkable dark clothes. Chained to his left wrist was a portfolio, while his right hand grasped a pistol at the ready.

The pistol was unexpected . . . but this was a first run, so in the excitement of the moment nobody thought to question its usefulness, accepting it as a forgivable precaution. What counted was that, if asked to swear to his identity, they would all have declared him to be the person they were awaiting: George E. Gunther, who had preceded the present trade counselor as head of intelligence at this embassy before being recalled to participate in the poster application program.

The name "poster" had been selected after much debate as adequately misleading, by analogy with "tanks" in the First World War and "tuballoy" in the Second.

Tension evaporated as the cabinet's door slid open, accompanied by a metallic and electrical smell; the transfer had required a great deal of power at both ends. Right hand outstretched, the ambassador strode forward.

"George, it's great to see you again! I guess there's no point in asking if you had a good trip, because—"

He broke off. Gunther's eyes had narrowed with suspicion and his gun was levelled at the ambassador's navel.

"George!" cried the first secretary. "Is something wrong?"

"Countersign!" Gunther hissed through tight-drawn lips.

"What countersign?" the ambassador demanded. "Nobody warned us you were instructed to require one!"

"Then I have been intercepted!" Gunther cried, and without a heartbeat's worth of hesitation turned his pistol on himself, while at the same time a thermite charge exploded in his portfolio, destroying the secret data it contained.

And incidentally wrecking the poster as efficiently as any saboteur's bomb.

TWO

suppose you wanted
to talk to the stars
and you succeeded
but it turned out
the stars themselves
are not on speaking terms

Being relatively small and relatively recent—it had been founded in the thirties by a millionaire whose fortune survived the Depression—Chester University was also relatively unknown. Eight years earlier, when telling his friends that he was taking up a post there, Justin Williams had met with blank looks, partly because few people had heard of the place, partly because he was forbidden to describe what he was going there to work on, and even if it had been allowed he would probably have been met with mockery.

But at least he had been able to say, "You know! Same place they run Project Ear."

At which their faces would light up. Everybody had heard about that latest of several attempts to detect messages from the stars, surviving to everyone's amazement when project after fundamental research project was being cancelled in the name of economy.

He had other cause to be grateful for its existence. Since he was still banned from discussing his own work save in the most general and misleading terms, he had often found it convenient to let strangers assume he was involved with Ear, having no difficulty in con-

veying that impression because the few friends he had
made at Chester actually did work on it, and kept him
up to date. Attempts to classify or restrict news of it
had long ago foundered on the intransigence of its director.

But he was dead now, and the vultures had closed in.

Daily since his arrival here Justin's drive to and
from work had carried him along a two-mile overpass,
separating through traffic from the city-center slums
where almost the only splash of color was provided by
billboards bearing patriotic slogans and pictures of Congressman Chester. From it there was a fine view of the
range of low hills to the west crowned with the antennae
of Project Ear's four-kilometer radio-telescope array.

Today in the morning sunlight polished girders
shaped to a fraction of a degree of curvature were being
not so much dismantled as hacked apart by a great
ungainly bird-shaped machine whose hammer head was
tipped with the slashing beak of an electric arc.

A carrion-eater. A fit surrogate for the man who
had ordered this desecration: T. Emory Chester.

Over the hum of the sparse morning traffic—several
self-guiding buses, a few cars, no "gas-guzzlers", by
order—Justin heard the clang and clatter as one especially heavy girder plunged to earth. His car was too
old to boast automatic routing; he was glad the need
to steer prevented him from looking that way.

Once, Project Ear had been a symbol of his own
ambitions. When he left college he had promised himself that one day he would make that sort of mark on
the world.

And he was doing so. But not in the manner he
would have chosen: instead, privately, deviously, under
government security restrictions and at the dictates of
a man he loathed.

Until very lately he had not been aware how much
he hated T. Emory Chester, grandson of the univer-

sity's founder. He owed him everything, above all the chance to prove that a hypothesis inconceivable a generation ago—for it was due to exhaustive computer evaluation of the original postulate—could be converted into functional machinery. Last year he would hotly have defended Chester—had done so, arguing with staffers from Project Ear who claimed he was trying to shut it down. Along with everyone else Justin had made compromising noises about satellites being preferable, the need to site detectors clear of all possible human signals, and so forth. Since it had been proved, though, that for less than the cost of launching a satellite these antennae could be automated, and since their life-expectancy was about half a century, he had imagined the worst that might happen would be the firing of a few of his acquaintances—unpleasant at a time of high unemployment, but not fatal.

He had never expected Chester to demolish everything when he won over the dean and faculty to his view that here was an unproductive application of his grandfather's fortune. Notionally the money was administered by an impartial trust; in practice Chester—who, like many who have inherited great wealth, craved the exercise of power he owed to no one but himself—was able to cajole, and wheedle, and browbeat, and if all else failed probably blackmail the trustees into agreeing with him. He ruled the Chester roost.

And he would not even consider the possibility of automating the project. In private he dismissed it as on all fours with astrology; in public—he was a frequent speaker at Department of Defense fund-raising events —as a waste because it did not contribute to national security. He wanted it torn down and the metal sold for scrap. He got his way, and the sole reason for Chester U to be famous vanished with every peck of that flaring electric beak.

The project which was going to ensure continuance

of DoD support was not mentioned in the media, ever
. . . that being Justin's own.

Sometimes, he thought bitterly, Chester reminded
him more than anybody of the Moslem warlord who
burned the great library of Alexandria, on the grounds
that if the manuscripts therein agreed with the Koran
they were superfluous, and if they disagreed they were
heretical.

The perimeter of the university was walled and its
points of access were under armed—and, more im-
portantly, computerized—surveillance. Justin halted his
car at the usual gate before the accusing eyes of a small
crowd of men and women in shabby clothes, doubtless
lured here by one of the recurring and always false
rumors that paid volunteers were wanted for some research project or other. All of them, whether black
or white, looked somehow grey, the color of long de-
privation. Half seemed approving of his car because it
was compact and old, half ready to spit at it because it
was foreign. He drove a 1980 Volvo which he could
well have afforded to change long ago, but which
showed no sign of wearing out. Besides, it was approved by the security branch of DoD as adequately
inconspicuous and typical of an academic.

He admitted himself to the campus by inserting his
identity card in a sensor-slot. Accepted, it was printed
with a one-time electronic code entitling him to park
in the lot outside Wright & Williams Inc. and enter his
own office, provided he did so in not more than fifteen
minutes. The world was undergoing another of its
cyclical waves of paranoia. Perhaps this one would
wash Chester up on the shores of the presidency if it
lasted out the decade; he was ambitious enough.

But at all events they were talking about having
next year's identity cards attached to an explosive
thread, which would melt them into unrecognizability
if they were snatched.

Sighing, Justin locked and left his car, making sure he was in plain sight of the guard on duty in the overseer's tower, and approached the headquarters of Wright & Williams Inc. It had never seemed proper to him that a commercial company should operate on university land, but there were others here not dissimilar, especially in the behaviorist-controlled psychology faculty. He was fairly sure DoD money was being spent there, too, but he had no proof.

Glancing up at the building's almost windowless façade, Justin wondered what would happen if Dean Shafto himself, let alone an inquisitive student, were to try and gain admission unannounced. The men and women who guarded the place were soldiers in plain clothes assigned on a random basis by the DoD, having no connection with the university, while even the staff he and his partner Cinnamon Wright worked with were picked not by them but by computers at the DoD, and were military or career civil service personnel. Not, of course, that that meant they were incompetent. In times like these some of the best university graduates looked at the figures for unemployed Ph.D.'s and settled for security in the one area where employment was actually increasing.

How the people at the top reconciled that fact with their cuts in every other area of public spending, Justin had long ago given up trying to figure out.

Once more, as he crossed the threshold, he offered up his identity card and thought about the mass of circuitry which was (how to frame it in words?) *glancing* at him.

And was glad this near-intelligence could not literally read his mind, as currently-fashionable jokes pretended. Lately he had heard a dozen such—for example: "I can't get to see my shrink any more, goddammit! I went in his office the other day as usual, and that dumb-

bell of a machine he keeps for a receptionist decided I
was cured and gave me a bill for twenty thousand!"

Justin felt the reverse of cured. He felt he had acquired a problem he didn't deserve. What could have
possessed him to walk into this kind of trap?

Oh, he remembered perfectly that at the time taking
DoD money, with Chester's sponsorship, really had
been the sole way of turning his brilliant inspiration into
a career. When he sent his one and only published
paper on the poster principle to a carefully-selected
journal known for its hospitality to *avant-garde* ideas
and its willingness to reprint lengthy computer analyses
of the type known jokingly as "yet another four-color
problem"—after the classic computer-exhaustive list of
solutions to that classic poser in topology—he had been
firmly convinced that it would instantly be recognized
as a breakthrough. He had dared to hope it might be
called a work of genius.

If it did nothing else, though, he would have been
content to have it act as his admission card (the image
was pervasive) to a university career, where he would
have plenty of friends working in research and plenty
of stimulating students.

Indeed he had seen at least a little of that secondary
ambition fulfilled, for just the kind of people he looked
forward to befriending had been working on Project
Ear.

Had. Past tense. Now thanks to Chester they were
scattering. Leaving Justin behind, with his guaranteed
funding, his infuriating partner, his single stroke of
genius unknown to the world at large, and almost
literally nobody to talk to. Being of a solitary temperament, he had expected to go on being resigned to
comparative loneliness all his life. But how different
the world looked from the vantage-point of thirty-four,
compared with twenty-six! How much less bearable!

What it amounted to was this: he had become a weapon, and against his will.

The moment he stepped out of the elevator on the office level—the computers were above and the poster lab above that—Justin realized this was going to be no ordinary Monday morning.

Cinnamon should not have been in the reception area. Nor should that man—what was his name? Bunker . . . ? No! Bulker!

For he was one of the immense entourage with which Chester surrounded himself. Machinery had grown cheap, even very complex and elaborate machinery. It was the proof of vast riches to purchase people instead. Chester would have made a good slave-owner. In this period of rising unemployment he had signed up scores of aides and servants. He was far from exceptional. Heirs to the older fortunes which were still multiplying cancerously on the world's stock-exchanges were acting like medieval British barons and recruiting what amounted to private armies.

But Bulker was among the most dislikable of Chester's hirelings. Why in hell were he and Cinnamon here, as it were lying in ambush?

He sought for clues in his partner's face. Wright and Williams were almost diametric opposites; she was as tall as him, but where he was stocky—and growing plump—she was lean. One day she would be gaunt. He was fair and blue-eyed; she was everywhere dark. Under a close-cropped head of tight-curling hair she displayed features like her African ancestors' ceremonial masks: square vertical forehead, deep eyes, broad nose, angular jaw. Today, as ever, she wore garb which announced that she didn't give a damn for her appearance and had the incidental advantage of matching the national mood: a blue shirt torn at one elbow, faded blue pants, old shoes on bare feet.

He had known her since the week before meeting

Chester. She had tracked him down as a result of the publication of his—now unobtainable—paper about the poster principle, in what started as a fit of fury and ended up as an uneasy partnership. She had been the only other person in the country, probably in the world, working along analogous lines. His ideas and hers had matched like coffee and cream, like ham and eggs, and because of her he found all other women boring, and most of the time nowadays he wished they had never met, because she had pre-empted half his life and given nothing in return. He had never dared so much as put his arm around her for fear of being rewarded with a roundhouse blow. Her upbringing, like his, discounted personal involvement. He had been briefly married while in college; it had not worked. It was presumable that she was not a virgin, either. But so far as long-term relationships went he admitted he might as well have been, and he was virtually certain the same applied to her.

Today she was changed. Never had he seen such an expression on her face: as though her skin had been drawn outward, compressing the flesh on her bones until she seemed desiccated, leaving her teeth bare in a feral scowl, her forehead ridged like a field new-ploughed, her eyes in a pumpkin-ghost glare.

He was so startled, he was unable to speak before Bulker said in a cool reproving tone, "Dr. Williams, we've been trying to reach you for nearly twenty-four hours."

"So? I never answer the phone on weekends!"

Even to himself, Justin's tone sounded like bluster.

"But this is a rather special weekend. It was the one the Defense Department chose to post a live agent overseas for the first time."

A great chill closed on Justin's heart. But he retorted, "So? We've posted live people before. Cinnamon's been posted—and so would I but for the chance of a coin that came down heads!"

That wasn't something he believed in his heart. At all costs they would have prevented him from running that risk. Even so . . .

"You don't believe," Bulker said musingly, "that anything could have gone wrong?"

Justin gazed at Bulker's inhumanly calm face. "You mean—?"

"I mean something big and bad went wrong, and Mr. Chester wants to discuss it with you personally. You'd better not keep him waiting any longer!"

THREE

what if when you castled
you found a weak square
what if when you castled
you found out about cannon
what if when you castled
you found it was in Spain

Deciding to build his family home on a bluff overlooking an inlet of the sea, the founder of the Chester fortune had instructed his architect to model it on a European castle. In an age when assassination was once again a constant risk for any public figure, his grandson had converted it into a true fortress. At either end of the terrace where he received his unwilling visitors this morning, anti-projectile radars hummed in ornamental turrets.

He was finishing a late breakfast in company with Zena di Cassio, the dark-haired woman a few years older than himself who might or might not be his mistress but had certainly been his confidante and counselor since before he took an interest in Justin and Cinnamon. Perhaps it had been at her suggestion he had done so; he had acquired a vast populist following by boasting that he had never learned to handle computers more complicated than the sort of pocket calculator he had been obliged to use in school, and even to make a phone call he issued orders to a servant.

Yet he was by no means blind to the impact of new technology. He had taken an immense gamble when he decided to back two young scientists with an invention most of their colleagues were dismissing out of hand, for either he or possibly Zena had foreseen that if the poster could be made to work, even though a single operation of it might cost millions—ruling it out for commercial exploitation—it must still have a revolutionary effect. Why should he care about making a profit from it? He had more money than he could ever spend. But there were governments which might be cowed into negotiation by a handful of saboteurs; there were others which might be overthrown by infiltrating half a hundred soldiers. That was the kind of power he one day wanted to wield. Money-power he had grown up with. Now he was in his late thirties he found it boring.

Therefore what had happened to Gunther disturbed him greatly. Numerous tests at shorter ranges had shown no ill-effects on human beings, while hundreds of similar transmissions, many over intercontinental distances, had safely transferred non-living consignments. Now that a poster had been developed capable of withstanding free-space radiation, there was to be an attempt to transfer matériel to and from orbit: the device's first potentially economic application.

Everything, in short, had seemed to be going splendidly—until this weekend. He looked forward with grim anticipation to hearing what Cinnamon and Justin had to say.

They were always nervous in his presence. He liked that. But today they were visibly angry, too. Better still! He invited them to sit down and take coffee, and as soon as their cups were filled gave a pre-arranged signal.

Moving to a control-board set in the side of the house, Bulker touched a series of switches. The breakfast-table and its burden of crockery slid silently away to the kitchen, while a roof-panel shut out the sky and a wall in which were set holographic screens rose to meet it on the seaward side. Diffuse lighting, very dim after the brilliance of sunlight, bathed them in a shadowless luminance as though they were under water.

The moment the transformation was complete, Chester demanded in a harsh voice, "You've been told what's happened?"

Justin licked his lips. "Only that something went wrong with the first live agent transfer," he muttered. "But the whole operation should have been straightforward."

"So it should." Chester leaned back in his chair, elbows on its arms, fingertips together. "Unfortunately the agent sent was very different from the agent who arrived."

There was a long stunned pause. Eventually Cinnamon said, "You mean he looked like someone else?"

"Not at all. He looked the same, sounded the same, and so far as they can make out from his corpse he was the same. But he acted wrong. The moment he arrived he demanded a countersign. None had been arranged. He shot himself and destroyed his courier's bag."

"But that's incredible!" Justin exclaimed.

"Isn't it?" Chester's tone was sardonic. "As yet I don't have a copy of the recording they made of his arrival, though naturally I've asked for one and I'll play it for you as soon as it gets here. What I have been told, though, is that he said, 'I've been intercepted!'"

"Out of the question," Cinnamon said at once.

"Why are you so sure?"

"Just think what an interception would involve! The power-throughput alone, to start with. We have to synchronize transmitter and receiver with atomic-frequency clocks and a satellite relay chiefly to keep down the time we need to apply full power. To snatch something in transit you'd need to be able to bring up another receiver, absolutely congruous with the right one, from zero to full power in the moment between dispatch and reception, and because as near as we can calculate that's one, count it *one,* chronon it's impossible. Otherwise you'd have to keep your receiver on standby for at least several seconds. The materials don't exist to make that feasible. The poster would melt!"

"But you're talking about something that hasn't happened," murmured Zena. She was sitting, as ever, at Chester's right and a little further away. "I imagine Dr. Williams has been listening to Emory's description of what *did* happen." She gave a smile full of brilliant white teeth.

Cinnamon, stung by the insult, came near to explosion—and then Zena's point dawned on her. Biting her thumb, she slumped back scowling in her chair.

Hastily Justin said, "Surely the point is that he wasn't intercepted, which is—as Cinnamon says—impossible, but that he thought he had been . . . You say he shot himself?"

"With an issue pistol. His own. They checked the number."

"Because when he didn't get a nonexistent countersign he thought he'd been intercepted? Who by—a foreign power?"

"I've told you the story as I heard it. Well?"

There was a long silence during which Justin and Cinnamon gazed up at the roof-panel. It was a pleasant and uniform blue, a cloudless sky for use on cloudy days.

After a while Cinnamon said musingly, "Did this agent express any doubts about the security of the system? Did he, for example, insist on his own initiative that there be a countersign at the receptor end, and did someone simply omit to warn the embassy?"

"That was the first thing we thought of," said Zena. "It's being investigated. So far the results are negative. There was no reason to doubt the secureness of the system, was there?"

"Even though there may be now."

Chester uttered his comment delicately, and again signalled to Bulker. Images began to appear on the holographic screens. With increasing dismay Justin and Cinnamon recognized themselves, mostly in Chester's company, and recalled the events depicted.

That was when they signed up for Chester Foundation money. That was when they were running early tests on their pilot model, capable of transmitting mere grams of matter over mere meters of distance. That was the first poster large enough to accept a human being. That was Cinnamon the day she was posted from end to end of the university campus, not the first volunteer because she was too precious to risk, but the fifth . . .

The series continued, featuring DoD officials.

Justin blurted, "I didn't know about these records!"

"We have the sound as well," Chester murmured. "The tape contains numerous declarations by both of you that nobody else could be working along the same lines, no one in any other country was even investigating the principle, no scientific papers were being published that so much as hinted at . . . *Et cetera.* A person in my position is often the target for confidence tricksters, you know. Therefore I always prepare for the worst."

"That's monstrous!" Cinnamon cried, jumping to her feet. "Confidence trick—*confidence trick?* Ask the Diplomatic Corps how many batches of secret data have been safely posted! Ask the Space Agency why they've invested half a billion!"

"You're missing the point again," Chester said. "The first time—the very first time—a major field mission is undertaken using the poster, something goes so wrong that the agent dies and his courier's bag is destroyed! Are you pleased? Are you satisfied?"

The double question struck chill into Cinnamon and Justin. It was culled from the campaign speeches which had secured Congressman Chester his unexpected majority over a liberal incumbent. Every time he addressed the sort of dissatisfied middle-class-on-the-way-down voters he hoped to recruit, he would list what the current administration had done since being elected, and at every point where they could be charged with failing the electorate that would be his cry to the audience.

Now he was in Congress, some of his colleagues were copying it. It had become a catch-phrase.

"I guess we better undertake some more live tests," Justin said at length, and Cinnamon gave a weary nod.

"Indeed you will," Chester said grimly. "As of today. I already told Levi Tesch to arrange a supply of volunteers matched to the previous ones. And this time there are going to be more physical examinations. The Navy is assigning a doctor called Baumgartner. Also a bunch of people from DoD and the Diplomatic Corps will be here tomorrow or the next day, including some of Gunther's former associates, and the *Lord* knows how we are going to explain away their interest in Chester U!"

The sudden emphasis was testimonial to a hundred meetings he had addressed in the Bible Belt. Cinnamon, who had been raised there and escaped, rose to her feet.

"Sure! You don't want anybody to notice that you're fixing on shifting H-bombs through the poster one of these days!"

"Messy," Chester said. "Obsolete. A nation which can only survive at the expense of exterminating its rivals is a failure. That would reduce us to the level of the enemy. Out-fighting is what savages believe in. Out-smarting is the civilized approach."

Abruptly he leaned forward, clenching his fists.

"Which is why I started to support you eight years ago! I would not enjoy learning that I'd been led up a dead end! You understand me? I set out to place your invention at the service of our great country, and I believed I'd done so—only a loyal agent is dead for no good reason! Will the same happen to the Marines we send to restore order, the Rangers who go to organize a trustworthy force in a foreign land . . . ? Hell, I shall be *extremely* angry if it turns out I'd have done better to let the commies have it!"

Zena, at full stretch, tapped his shoulder. The pressure went out of him. "Get back to your damned laboratory, then," he grumbled. "And don't let me down twice!"

Justin scrambled to his feet, his mind full of visions of those vast and graceful antennae he had passed this morning, being reaped as by the scythe of death.

FOUR

*eliminate the impossible
and whatever is left
however improbable
must be the truth
yes but suppose that
one time nothing remains*

Ill-tempered, Justin and Cinnamon sat side by side at a table in the poster hall which occupied the whole of the top floor of the Wright & Williams building, studying the readouts which appeared on screens before them as members of the technical staff tested circuit after circuit not only in the prototype poster which occupied the center of the floor but also in the walls and ceiling. Entering this room was like being swallowed by a beast, particularly since the cybernetics engineers had taken to using biological terms for their connections: villi, vibrissae.

Abruptly Cinnamon slapped the table and shoved back her chair.

"We're wasting time!" she declared. "What's the use of checking our equipment? If they let us get our hands on the machine they used to post Gunther we might do some good, but . . ."

"Do you really think so?" Justin countered sourly.

She hesitated, then sighed. "I guess not," she muttered, turning away. "How the hell could being posted drive someone crazy? I mean, he got to where he was meant to go, right?"

"Maybe poster-phobia is latent in the human species," Justin offered, "and nobody could know about it until we built the machines which sparked it off."

"Then why didn't the volunteers—?" she began before realizing he was putting her on. Furious, she was about to give him a piece of her mind when the elevator door opened and they both glanced reflexively towards it.

Immediately they recognized Professor Major Levi Tesch, who insisted on being addressed by both his titles—in that order—whenever the Army activated his reserve commission in the Medical Corps. He held the chair of psychology and psychiatry at a Mid-Western university. Dark-haired, sallow and with heavy glasses, he was obviously in a foul mood. That was no surprise. He had agreed to test the first—military—volunteers to go through the poster, in the expectation of boasting about how he was in on the ground floor of that new invention which was transforming the world. As he put it, it was like standing in the sand dunes at Kittyhawk.

But immediately he realized he was banned from discussing what he had learned he stormed off, announcing he would never return to Chester U.

Somehow they had put enough pressure on him to make him break his word.

With him was a thin brown-haired man, a stranger, whom he urged in the direction of Justin and Cinnamon. Having exchanged perfunctory handshakes, he dropped into a nearby chair and nodded at his companion.

"This is Colonel Lane. Apparently he dispatched the agent who killed himself. Beyond that deponent sayeth not, except that if you have a drink it would come welcome."

Levi was in one of his outrageous moods, Justin realized. He rose, waving Lane to a chair, and presented himself.

"I'm Justin Williams and this is my partner Cinnamon

Wright, and Levi knows perfectly well that liquor is not allowed on our premises. What can we do for you?"

"We were just talking about what you ought to be doing for us," Cinnamon cut in, resuming her own chair. "Like letting us at the poster you used to send Gunther abroad!"

Lane took his time over composing himself into a comfortable position, and at length looked up at her with a steady gaze.

"Since the poster we used, Dr. Williams, was as exact a copy of the pilot model as we could possibly achieve, if it was a machinery fault which led to poor George's fate, it's as likely to be identified here as elsewhere. My own department's engineers are currently evaluating our poster, just as you are. Am I to take it that you think it is a machinery fault we're looking for?"

The gibe was quiet but perfectly aimed. Cinnamon shook her head angrily and stared off into space, ignoring the others. In a placatory tone Justin said, "Frankly, Colonel, we see no way that could have happened. Professor Tesch will confirm what I say."

"Right," Tesch said morosely. "They've dragged me here to go through the same motions as before—they've even matched the so-called volunteers the same as last time, two male and two female, two black and two white—and I know even before I start administering my tests I'll get the same results from all of them before and after being posted. I wish I could get on with it! But there's some Navy doctor or other running physical checks and he says he'll be at it most of the day."

Lane leaned back and crossed his legs, very much at ease. "Did you know George Gunther?" he inquired. "No? Nor you, Dr. Williams—Dr. Wright?"

Headshakes.

"I did know him. He was an old friend. He was a loyal and enterprising agent. Nowhere on his record is there the slightest hint that he might kill himself. I am determined to find out why he did so the first time he was transmitted by your invention. I hope that's clear!"

Sudden menace colored his last sentence. The others shrugged and nodded.

"So!" Lane sat upright again. "First, tell me whether I'm keeping you from anything urgent."

"No, it's being done for us," Cinnamon muttered.

"What, precisely?"

Justin intervened. "These people are interrogating the circuitry of the entire poster hall, putting what might look like nonsense questions. They aren't nonsense; they're carefully designed to produce specific answers. If they don't, we can be sure there's an error somewhere."

Lane nodded. "Yes, I understand. We use the same techniques. So if it wasn't a machine fault that killed George Gunther . . . ?"

Cinnamon snorted and went on elaborately disregarding him. Justin said after a moment, "We were told we could see a recording of what happened."

"You will. Soon as it gets here. It's being brought by hand, of course. But why is that so crucial?"

"Well—" Justin spread one hand in the air. "For one thing, we don't understand why he was carrying a gun. How he could have imagined he might be intercepted . . . !"

Lane allowed himself a frown. "Yes, that's where we're stuck, to be frank."

Cinnamon, stirring, said suddenly, "Had he told anyone he wanted a countersign on arrival?"

"We've been over that," Lane sighed. "The answer seems to be no."

"What about eddy currents?" Levi said unexpectedly.

They all glanced at him uncomprehendingly.

"Eddy currents!" he repeated in an irritable tone, sitting upright. "The brain operates on microvolt signals, right? Suppose Gunther had subconscious reservations about your claim that this is the world's most secure transportation system. Suppose it was on his mind that he ought to guard against being hijacked. Suppose he departed knowing that he hadn't mentioned the idea to anyone, and arrived firmly believing that he had. It would take only the tiniest shift in his neural flow—"

"It doesn't fit," Cinnamon interrupted with forceful certainty. "We checked that out well in advance of the first human tests. We sent through delicate electronic equipment operating on current even smaller than the brain, and we got to the stage where we could start a program running before dispatch and read the answer after delivery. We never had a single error."

"But what about sub-threshold error?" Lane said sharply. "If you're duplicating the object in transit at the receptor end—"

"But we *aren't!*" Cinnamon exploded. "It's not a question of duplicating! The laws of the universe wouldn't permit that much information to be transmitted that accurately! We imitate the space around the object!"

"You haven't met these people before," Levi said, giving Lane a skeletal grin. "They aren't scientists. They're magicians. They invent terms as and when they need to. What's rho-space? It's where the object goes which is being shifted from transmitter to receptor at the speed of light! *I* was told that something moving that fast would acquire infinite mass. Yes, they say, so it must. So where's the mass? It manifests as energy. Now just a moment, I say! You're using a lot of energy for the transfer, but it isn't infinite! Of course not, they say. The surplus doesn't even show up as heat. Of course not, they say. Where is it? It's in rho-space, they say. Are you any the wiser? I swear to God I'm not!"

Hearing this caricature of the elegant theory which it had cost him a year of sleepless nights to formalize to the stage where he could commit investigation of its implications to a computer, Justin was on the verge of boiling over. Cinnamon for once came to his rescue.

"That's just it! It doesn't take infinite energy to deform space! You're doing it, I'm doing it, any solid object, just by *existing*. The presence of energy sufficient to make the two spaces congruent ensures that whatever is in the full one makes the trip to the empty one and the process would continue indefinitely except that we now have the nanosecond computer reflexes to stop it when it suits us. The contents of the two volumes shuttle and we cancel the congruence on an odd-numbered phase of the node-pattern!"

"Simple!" said Levi in precisely the tone he would have used for the payoff line of a classic Yiddisher joke.

Cinnamon threw her hands in the air and jumped to her feet. Justin braced himself for an outburst of rage, but at that moment the elevator opened again and a man emerged who looked not unlike Levi except that he was a trifle taller and instead of being lank his hair was curly.

Levi rose reluctantly.

"This is Captain Herman Baumgartner," he said. "Who is, I guess, through with the volunteers by now?"

"Sure," the newcomer said, parking a medical bag—containing fewer instruments than computer-compatible sensors—on the handiest flat surface. "Sorry to have kept you hanging around. Frankly, I don't know why they called me in. Whatever happened to that poor guy Gunther, it wasn't a cerebral hemorrhage or a heart-attack!"

"Right," Levi said. "And now I have to put them through my professional hoops—quizzes and tests and tests and quizzes—and I know exactly what's going to happen. Even the computers are going to tell me that the only difference between the answers they give before being posted and after being posted can be ascribed to the novelty of the experience."

"Well, they're fit enough at all events," Baumgartner said. "Sometimes seems to me that only the services can afford to give people a decent diet and a decent physical régime these days . . . Here they come now, I guess."

The elevator was cycling again, and delivering the four volunteers accompanied by a Marine guard. Armed, of course. Wright & Williams Inc. existed in a very paranoid situation. But Levi had insisted last time, and doubtless was insisting again, that his subjects take their tests in the surroundings they were to be posted to from the other side of the campus.

The white woman out of the four was fortyish and four-square, while the black one was a few years younger and much slimmer. Looking at her, Justin felt a pang of crazy insight. Maybe before she was transferred someone should take her to bed and run a kind of Masters & Johnson evaluation, and then repeat the process afterwards. Maybe some significant change would show up.

But who could one trust to undertake the task—a superstud with a thousand pubic scalps to his credit? The notion faded as rapidly as it had come, and the technicians returned to report just what he had expected: everything was apparently in normal working order.

It was slender consolation to be assured that his brainchild was perfect when a man was dead because of it.

FIVE

how disconcerting it is
when you trust your weight
to a stepping-stone
and suddenly feel it
settle deeper
in the bed of the stream

Forty-eight hours of constant striving with minimal sleep reduced their nerves to shreds. It was hard for Justin to decide whether it was worse for himself, whose sole claim to a place in the history-books was at stake; or for Cinnamon, who had had to digest the bitter pill of arriving second, yet had valiantly applied herself to the engineering side of the project and helped turn it into reality; or for Levi, whose subtlest personality-testing procedures were being called in question thanks to a problem that was none of his responsibility; or for Herman Baumgartner, who had suddenly been pitch-forked into something which last week he had not even suspected the existence of.

Come to that, it was probably not much fun for the volunteers, who were as a matter of policy kept in complete ignorance of what was being done to them.

The one person for whom Justin felt no sympathy at all was the one who turned up at the head of a string of aides—so-called—and in company of Colonel Lane when the situation in the labs was approaching boiling point. Without the least intention he and Cinnamon were on the verge of yet another stand-up row, and the helplessness he felt whenever such a crisis developed

29

was magnified until it was almost intolerable now that for once their common future was in the balance.

Among the instrumentation it had been deemed apposite to incorporate in the poster hall were medical detectors which assessed the condition of its occupants by assaying anthropotoxins and other incidental metabolic substances. Red lights had been flashing for the past hour when Chester and his companions strode in.

It was not the happiest augury for tomorrow.

Often in the past Justin had thought of the personnel assigned to the firm by "higher authority" as the walking, talking equivalent of interchangeable spare parts. It was no special surprise to him, therefore, when as he looked up wearily from the latest of uncountable printouts confirming that all was functioning as intended he discovered he could not remember the name of the person who was saying in an awed tone, "Mr. Chester and Ms. di Cassio are here to see you!"

He knew only that any interruption was a welcome one.

Rising, smiling at Lane because so far the colonel had done him no personal affront—and moreover had lost a friend when Gunther died—he went through the automatic motions of providing chairs, except for the "aides" who took station bodyguard-fashion near the door and looked around uneasily as though in search of windows, too, which the poster hall did not possess, and signalled Levi and Herman to come and join him. Cinnamon, scowling incredibly, marched away to the water-cooler and after drinking leaned on it, breathing hard.

Mentally Justin crossed his fingers. Given another minute or two she would boil down her accumulated rage to a handful of well-honed insults, and after that things would be as near normal as they ever were.

But more and more red lights were flickering on the medical monitoring panel. Were this a nuclear facility, their intensity would long ago have triggered the scram warning.

He noticed on Zena's face a sort of Mona Lisa smile which hinted she was not entirely unhappy with the situation.

The hell with her . . .

Struggling against all odds to act like the chairman and managing director of a firm called Wright & Williams Inc.—and, moreover, an inventive genius who would ultimately be remembered if not with Einstein and Newton then at least with Cayley and Watt—Justin bustled around hostess-fashion, calling for coffee and soft drinks, until all of a sudden he realized that Cinnamon had ceased to lean on the water-cooler and was fixing him with a beady, critical eye.

Her expression was so pregnant with the threat of storms, he relapsed into his chair with a shrug and let Chester do precisely what he had intended from the moment he entered: dominate the company.

"*Thank* you, Dr. Williams . . ." That, with a kind of silky nastiness. As ever, he was dressed up for this confrontation; unkind critics would have termed his gear old-fashioned, for it was a dark suit, a white shirt, a gold tie, and it had been years since except at the most formal functions any male wore a tie. Women sometimes did, but never with a shirt.

Justin supposed it was a signal that the wearer was harking back to the good old values of the past. What was good about them? Nobody so far had explained that to him . . .

"I take the extraordinary step—"

Fatigue making him hyper-alert, Justin tensed, finding his eyes drawn to Zena. He went on listening, registering each successive word as though it were being told off on a score-board.

"—of accompanying Colonel Lane here to your laboratory because—"

Justin narrowly avoided giving a meaning nod. He

was on the track of something which would make far
better sense than the words Chester was mouthing.

"—not only has it transpired that a loyal agent of
our great and beloved country—"

Mm-hm! This was the Old Glory bit being trotted
out!

"—was condemned to a foul and loathsome death—"

Come on! Where's the but?

Justin was almost alarmed at the way he felt he was
reading the script in advance.

"—but—"

Sharp on time, baby!

"—as it turns out the only conceivable reason for
his fate—"

Just possibly Cinnamon was in step with him. Justin glanced at her. Her face was as frozen as the Greenland icecap. Too bad! Zena's face, on the other hand . . .

"—must be ascribed to a failure of the fundamental
design."

Yes. She wrote the script. Except that probably there
never was one. It was more compiled than written. It
was a case for the defense instead of an assessment of
the facts. Whatever had become of Gunther it must be
due to some flaw in his personality and not to a mistake
in the program for the complex computers which masterminded the transfer from poster A to poster B.

But because T. Emory Chester had staked his personal ambitions on providing the State Department and
the Department of Defense with a tool which in a
subtler fashion than H-bombs would enable them to rule
the world, this truth must be disguised. Any mistakes
must be blamed on available scapegoats. The fact that
the poster had already fulfilled the claims made for it in
the first place was now irrelevant.

That key word, "must", fluttered around Justin's
brain like a frightened bat, looking for a safe place to
settle for the winter of impending discontent.

Justin looked at Chester as he spoke and read in

his expression visible unhappiness. He looked at Zena and on her face found satisfaction plain to see. It made zero odds that the laws of nature brooked no appeal. Stalin told Lysenko to prove that evolution was subject to political necessity. A bill was introduced in the state legislature of Indiana to make *pi* equal to three. Same difference.

And what chance did he have to out-argue his opponents? Before that task Justin quailed. He well knew—and was ashamed to have to admit—that he himself did not wholly comprehend what happened when a poster was put into operation. It was his invention, certainly! But for the first time in history something had been conceived which exceeded the power of a human brain to analyze. He personally was reconciled to that eventuality, as the logical outcome of generations of technology. Piled like Pelion upon Ossa, it must . . .

There was the hateful word again: "must"!

But during the detour his mind had been taking other words had been spoken. Colonel Lane had picked up the tale; he was saying now, "—the project must have been sabotaged from the very beginning!"

Dead silence reigned in the poster hall, bar the hum of the tireless electronics.

Then Cinnamon erupted.

"You're insane! You're claiming that all the effort we sank into the poster was motivated by a desire to squander Defense Department money! Ah, *shit!* Go have your head shrunk, stop bugging us!"

Justin had always envied her ability to switch from mode to mode in a single breath.

Lane did not share his view. He said simply, "No."

"What then?" Cinnamon blinked at him.

"Defense Department money is irrelevant. The death of one of our best intelligence agents isn't. The fact we have to calculate with *is* . . . *!*"

He leaned forward, just as Zena gave an approving nod.

"Immediately your poster was used for the first time for an agent transfer, it drove him insane and killed him and destroyed the data he was carrying!"

"But it's a machine!" Cinnamon shouted. "Like a computer! GIGO—garbage in, garbage out! Was it *our* poster that sent Gunther to his death? Was it one *we* built? Hell, no! It was one you built, and are so ashamed of you won't even let us visit it!"

Suddenly dropping her voice by several decibels, she added, "Don't forget that everything which is said in here is recorded and phonetically transcribed. I stand by what I have thus far said without reconsideration."

As though the absurdity of Lane's charge had struck home, Justin was gratified to see both Zena and Chester flinch.

"Christ, it's like living in the Middle Ages!" Cinnamon concluded, spinning on her heel. "Thou God Seest Me! Only it's some paranoid computer program at the DoD dreamed up by thick-witted short-sighted pig-headed idiots like you"—with a stab of one long brown finger towards Lane—"and not God! You set out to put the worst possible interpretation on whatever anybody does! You decided that the enemy can outsmart you under any circumstances! And you're right! Why? Because the only thing that saves you from being totally stupid is the fact that you've noticed you're stupid! You're bound to lose, baby! *Bound* to lose!"

"Watch your tongue!" Lane snapped. "I'll have you up on a loyalty charge if—"

"Hey-hey!" Cinnamon crowed in high delight. "Just like I said! I was going to tell you go read the history of the rise of Fascism, in case you learned better from it. I was wrong, wasn't I? You don't have to be told anything about that. You do it automatically! See an intelligent person, an original thinker, you stamp on it fast! It could be harmful!"

Lane's face darkened. "One more word out of you and—"

"Here's your one more word," Justin cut in, rising to his feet. A chill sense of doom pervaded his body, but what Cinnamon had just said was so close to what had been brewing in his mind for years past, he would have been unable to face himself in the mirror had he not acted now.

"If I ever before regretted putting *my* invention, the poster, at the service of my country, I thought it was a fit of the blues, the spinoff from a bad dream. Not until I met *you*"—he spoke to Lane, but looked at Zena, and meant Chester, and knew that all the implications were registering—"did I ever guess I might regret being an inventor! Since you're accusing me of being a saboteur who has cunningly trapped everybody here into wasting public money on something which is actually designed to kill *loyal agents,* and since I can't imagine a filthier insult you could level at me, I insist on being posted myself, over at least the same distance as Gunther!"

There was a brief pause during which Justin learned, by the spreading smiles on the faces of Zena and Chester and eventually Lane, that he had once more misunderstood his fellow human beings.

"I'm delighted that you're willing to co-operate in Project Touchstone," Chester said at length, rising and beaming. "But, you understand, it must be in the reverse direction . . ."

SIX

it profits one
to cross the great water
to be a great man
but what shall it profit
to be without honor
to lose his soul

"Why did they let me out?"

A dozen times Justin almost—miraculously, never quite—spoke the question aloud as the airliner sped across the fleece-white fields of heaven under a brilliant sun. His blurted defiance had been meant as nothing more than a way of reminding everybody else present, in particular Chester, that the poster was his, not theirs.

Above all, he had never expected to be taken at his word. It was a condition of his contract with the Chester Foundation that he must not leave the confines of the continental United States. He had accepted that with resignation, certain that the prohibition would be waived later on if he requested it. Then, he had been thinking in terms of foreign scientific congresses, scarcely crediting that his achievement would be so totally concealed by security screens that the rest of the world would remain ignorant of it.

And that was precisely what should have brought him on this, his first trip to the Old World! He should be *en route* to deliver an address to a meeting of his colleagues, who would give him a standing ovation; he should be met with cheers and bouquets; he should pose at the head of the steps leading down from the plane with (he checked and interrogated himself on the next point, then continued with his vision, convinced it was right) Cinnamon on his arm, target for scores of Third World photographers who wanted her picture as evidence that black people too could be in the forefront of scientific advance.

But instead . . .

He had not considered the need to disguise the fact that he would not be returning the way he had come. *They* had. For the purposes of this trip he was Philip C. Parker, an independent businessman, who had spotted an export opportunity and on the spur of the moment applied for a passport and bought an airline ticket.

Mr. Parker, regrettably, was scheduled to have a heart-attack tomorrow at about eleven or twelve o'clock. His body would be flown home in a coffin.

Justin had not dared inquire how a suitable corpse had been obtained.

Every step of the way he had been under surveillance. Now, aboard the plane, he was conveniently seated next to an affable junior trade counselor from the embassy, who was full of admiration for anyone who was prepared to make this kind of trip on impulse and kept insisting that he call by the embassy tomorrow for help with the paperwork: "You know how it is in these socialist countries! Nothing gets done except in triplicate!"

But she was only the latest. Probably she would offer to share a cab with him from the airport into the city; if he declined, there would be someone next to him on the bus instead. It ought to have been reassuring to feel that *they* were taking such good care of him. It was the reverse. Why had they let him out at all?

Was it not because they judged his period of originality and creativity to be over?

He had dismissed that ridiculous charge of treason almost before it was uttered, and knew it was spawned of fatigue and frustration, like his retort. But if they expected him to create anything else important, would they have allowed him to go abroad at all?

And what if, by some incredible mischance, the enemy knew who he really was? He could still talk about the poster principle. He could be made to reveal his knowledge under torture. There could be secret police waiting in his hotel. Or on the bus. Or even here in the plane!

For just a few minutes, now and then, he had managed to look forward to this trip, thinking that if nothing else he might see unfamiliar sights, hear unfamiliar languages, enjoy unfamiliar food.

With the presence in the next seat of an embassy official the last hope of that evaporated. He would docilely do as he was told; he would go where they wanted him to go; tomorrow he would be posted home.

Of that, oddly, he was not at all afraid. He had talked to Cinnamon after her one and only trip through the poster, and she had been even curter than usual when she told him, "I get more of a trip from crossing a sidewalk!"

He was not Gunther. Who must have had some hidden personality flaw. He was the inventor of the poster principle. He had even at one point dreamed of being the first to pass through his creation from A to B . . . only *they* had interdicted him.

Perhaps he should have claimed it as of right.

The seat-belt sign came on. A cheerful voice announced it was overcast and raining at their destination. It had been raining when they took off, too.

Obediently clicking the buckle in his lap, Justin reflected on the paradox that if the poster were ever to become commonplace, its users would go straight from rainy day to rainy day, denied the sight of sun on bright white cloud.

It was not quite as bad as he had come to fear. The woman he had sat beside was met by an embassy car, but did not insist on him sharing it; he was allowed to ride the narrow, badly-sprung bus which delivered foreign visitors limousine-style to the various main hotels. The one he was assigned to was like something from a Victorian novel: all crystal chandeliers and gilt-and-plush chairs. Moreover it boasted an elevator which was completely unashamed of its function. It rose and fell with a clang of great iron chains. According to a brass plaque polished to near-illegibility it had been designed and installed by Hippolyte Masquinet, Lift-Maker, Paris, in 1888—or maybe 1886; the metal was so worn it was impossible to be sure.

A trifle awed, for not even at Chester's had he been among so many objects old enough to qualify as antiques which were still in daily use, Justin wondered against his will whether this Monsieur Masquinet had also dreamed of being remembered for revolutionizing transportation. When the only means of rising vertically were balloons and untrustworthy dirigibles, an elevator must have created quite a sensation . . .

There was nothing either old-fashioned or inefficient about the telephone in his room. It shrilled almost as soon as he shut the door behind the man who had carried his bags.

"Mr. Parker!"

It was the woman he had sat next to on the plane. Just as well she used his pseudonym—he had been on the point of answering with his usual, "Williams!"

"I had a word with my boss. Says he'd be pleased to meet you at about ten tomorrow. I hope that's okay by you. Get a good night's rest and recover from your jet-lag, hm? See you!"

Oh, well . . . !

But the advice was sensible; he intended only to stretch out for an hour to recover from the trip, but to his fury woke four hours later, when it was already local evening. Then the surveillance continued. When he went down to the bar with a raging thirst—reassured to find that the elevator operator, the barman and the rest of the staff spoke English—he was picked up with elegant finesse by a man in his thirties with a woman somewhat younger, who proved to be (?) an exporter on a twice-yearly visit, breaking in a new secretary to the firm's routine. This hotel, they explained, was popular with Western visitors because of its character and the fact that its food was above average. They invited him to share their table at dinner, plied him with an excellent local wine, and subsequently suggested that he accompany them to a cellar-club where a folk-band roared out traditional melodies and the floor was awash with the overflow from liter-sized steins of dark beer.

As he was turning in at one A.M. local, he realized that he had been very deftly taken care of . . . and enjoyed himself at the same time.

Why in the world, he wondered as he dropped off, could not the whole of his life be equally pleasant?

Had he not earned it?

The phone shrilled at nine, local time. Muzzily groping for it, he was reminded by the woman he had met on the plane about his date at the embassy at ten.

So his brief moment of freedom was over. Now he must be posted home, there to endure test upon physical and psychological test. The day before yesterday he had undergone all of them for comparison purposes.

It scarcely seemed worth travelling so far for such an anti-climax.

In the redoubt beneath the embassy, to which he was admitted only after exhaustive screening, he was obliged to remove his clothes, shoes, even wrist-watch. Of course; they were the property of Philip Parker, and must go home on his corpse. In place of them he was given an oversuit of acid green.

At least one human touch was permitted. When he emerged from the screen behind which he had changed clothes, he found the ambassador waiting. Who strode forward and clasped his hand, declaring, "Sir, it is a privilege to meet someone like yourself who is not only brilliant but also brave!"

Am I? Actually I think I'm a damned fool!

Buoyed up, nonetheless, by the accolade, Justin stepped into the brand-new poster cabinet. It had, of course, been tested in both directions. Crates and packages had been shuttling back and forth from here to home without the slightest fault since it was installed. In the whole room there was no trace of the thermite which had charred Gunther into a mess of roasted meat, bar a grey smear or two on the walls.

Was there a look of disappointment on the ambassador's face?

Yes, very probably. He would have expected the inventor of the poster to take a special interest in this new installation, ask to be shown over it, maybe insist on being allowed to interrogate the circuitry.

But what was the point? This poster wasn't designed by humans. It was at four removes from anything a human being could analyze. Organic brains simply did not possess the patience.

He stood upright, smiled, raised his hand in a sketch for a salute just as the wall-clock's hand closed on the zero hour. It was, locally, six minutes after noon.

And *blink*. He was in the poster hall at Chester U.

It worked! It really worked! It really did! Suddenly he believed in his guts that he was, after all, a genius.

SEVEN

climbing a ladder
in the dark
feeling a rung crack
remembering that by daylight
it was indistinguishable
from all the others

"Did you overdo things last night?" Levi murmured, studying his monitor screens.

Justin felt himself blushing. "You mean do I have a hangover?" he said after a moment.

"Let's just say some of these responses are off by a factor which lack of sleep alone wouldn't explain. Well?"

"Uh . . . I guess I do."

"Right, I'll get Herman to run blood and urine checks so I know how much to compensate by."

"Otherwise how am I?" Justin ventured.

"Same old Justin," Levi answered with a shrug, turning away. "All yours, Herman!" he added more loudly.

There was an air of celebration in the poster hall today. Everybody seemed to be in an excellent mood. Even Cinnamon had for once put on a dress: floor-length, in an eye-searing African print, it suited her marvellously. Possibly it was by way of defying Chester that she had donned it. It was an apt symbol, Justin thought. So far as he was concerned, the posting had gone faultlessly. Apart from the effects of too much beer, he felt fine. Gunther's fate *must* have been due to an accident—a tragic accident, but still an accident.

The like of which must never be allowed to occur again.

Peeling off his oversuit for Baumgartner's examination, he thought to ask, "Where's Chester?"

He had had the vague impression he was scheduled to be here.

Yawning, which reminded him with a start that these people had had to get up early to be ready for his arrival from a European noon, Cinnamon answered.

"Oh, still sweet-talking the brass at DoD, I guess. When we get through here, though, we're to go have dinner in a new restaurant that just opened west of town. If he can he'll meet us there; either way he picks up the tab."

"Feeling generous today?" Justin muttered. Baumgartner gave him a sharp glance.

"That's an odd way to talk about the guy who financed the whole poster project!"

"Sorry," Justin muttered, abashed. Of course: Baumgartner thought of Chester as the archetypal loyal citizen. Naturally he would, having only heard of him prior to his arrival here at the beginning of the week. "Tired, I guess," he added in extenuation.

"Mm-hm. Don't worry. Soon as we're through here, you can take a few hours' rest. Or I can give you something to wake you up for a while."

"I'd rather not."

"Suit yourself. Hold out your arm. This may hurt."

The tests were complete by four P.M. local and Justin was able to enjoy the promised rest. Woken, washed, shaved, dressed in clothes he found provided for him—less conservative than his usual taste, but a good fit, presumably bought in a hurry when someone remembered that his wardrobe for the role of "Philip Parker" had been left behind—he found himself looking forward to a square meal.

Since neither Levi nor Herman had a car here, and Cinnamon's was a two-seater, he offered to drive all four of them to the new restaurant—so new that he had never heard of it. On the way he was acutely aware of how untidy his car's interior had become; it was the kind of thing you didn't notice until someone else was given a lift and all kinds of miscellaneous junk had to be dumped in the trunk. He made a resolution to clean it out next chance he got. Also there was a whine in the transmission, to be investigated.

The restaurant was a complete surprise. It specialized in wholefoods, although—judging by its clientele—at the upper end of that market. This was very much to Justin's taste, but he would never have expected Chester to patronize such a place. Maybe it was because it had waiters and waitresses, which fitted his preference for buying people rather than machines. Most inexpensive restaurants had been driven to adopt automated delivery, with radar-controlled trolleys—the radar to stop them bumping into customers—conveying food from kitchen to table. It was a little like being carried back to yesterday, he observed as he salt-and-lemoned a can of *tecate* beer, and the remark loosed a flood of questions from all three of his companions, but above all from Levi, whose ancestors, it turned out, hailed from the very city he had so briefly visited.

Justin felt crestfallen at the poverty of his answers. To have travelled so far and seen so little . . . Still, he was able to raise a laugh or two with his description of Monsieur Masquinet the lift-maker, whom he presented as a fussy self-important little man convinced that ultimately his elevators would convey people to the moon. That having gone over well, he risked complaining about how he had been shepherded every meter of his journey, despite the presence of Herman who, as a career naval officer, might well have taken exception to even an implied criticism of the way the government took care of its citizens abroad.

Signalling their waiter, Herman confounded his expectations by grousing about the places he had visited aboard Navy ships without being able to go ashore and explore them properly. Justin cheered up and accepted a beer too many, precisely as he had done (last night?) the night before.

Whenever that was. He felt very full of lentil soup and organic vegetables and bread so delicious it would ruin anybody's starch-restricted diet, and being in the company of these unexpectedly agreeable people felt like an excellent way of celebrating his successful—but forever-to-be-secret—poster trip.

Maybe it was better this way. After all, had not the Wright brothers been scoffed at by all the newspapers bar one?

Of course it would have been better still had some of his friends from Project Ear been present . . . He ventured a remark about how sad a loss that was, but the others were temporarily concerned with another subject entirely, and Cinnamon—who was paying attention with half her mind—said something to the effect that as soon as things could be routinely posted up to orbit it could all be started over with a far better chance of success.

That wasn't what Justin meant, but he made no attempt to start an argument. What small intention he had of doing so was sabotaged by a colossal yawn.

"Hey, man!" Cinnamon said, checking her watch. "It's late! You must be tired. No chance of Chester joining us now. Levi, why don't you and Herman call a cab back to your hotel when you're ready? I'll drive Justin home."

"Sure," Levi said. "Poster-lag must be worse than jet-lag. Should have thought of that—sorry!"

"You have to go?" Herman said, blinking. "Damn! I wanted to talk to you some more. Always seemed to me kind of unjust a guy like you could hit on something as revolutionary as the poster and have to miss out on the sort of success other people get for far, far less because you can't patent a natural law."

"Yeah," Levi muttered. "Just as well, I guess, that Chester had a fortune already!"

That was only a fraction of the story, in Justin's view, but hearing the words gave him the same warm sensation he had had from the ambassador's fulsome compliment—which he had refrained from mentioning. Out of perverted modesty?

He shook hands with Levi and Herman, making imprecise promises to "do this again," and followed Cinnamon back to his car, which she took the wheel of with exactly the sort of infuriating universal competence he had long ago learned to expect from her.

During the ride he felt his head clear. That was a relief, because Cinnamon was stopping not at his place—ah, how could she? This was his car!—but at hers, so presumably he must drive on from here. He was ready to slide into the driving seat when she forestalled him.

"Coming in? Or are you totally wiped out? Because if you are you'd better come in anyway, right?"

A little confused by the logic, but excited by the invitation—since it was without precedent—he followed her up to her apartment. She had the top floor of a four-storey building, a single wide volume with a living area, a sleeping area and a cooking area, and a fine view almost but not quite to the edge of the sea. Everywhere he looked he saw things he would have guessed to be typical of her taste, from a pile of decorated African dishes made of calabash rind to—inevitably—her own terminal for the Chester U mainframe computer. As she slipped her ident card in the lock music had greeted them, gently rhythmical and almost sleepy, while lights came on at a low level to suit the hour.

"Fix yourself a drink if you want one," she said as she closed the door. "I have to go take a leak."

She strode across the immense room towards a maze of slatted bamboo screens at the far end, kicking off her shoes as she went. The floor was covered with a thick fleecy off-white carpet. Three dark-green seating units with two black-topped tables at the corners formed a square U in the center, the open end towards a grey stone console carrying a TV on a swivel base which was currently doubling as a melodochrome display to match the music; its beams were shifting through the autumn colors, dark green, russet and gold.

He was impressed. But it wasn't surprising that Cinnamon should live in such style.

Did he want a drink, even if he could find one? Very much he did not. He was already doubtful of his ability to drive home safely, what with *tecate* and poster-lag. Levi's neologism made him chuckle. However, being invited into Cinnamon's home was an event, and he must not waste it, for his head was buzzing with questions he had wanted to put to her all day, concerning Gunther and what could have afflicted him.

He headed for the square-U seating, found it extremely comfortable, and leaned back with the intention of closing his eyes for no more than a couple of seconds.

Drowsiness betrayed him. He was half asleep, deliciously, when he felt a hand stroke his hair. Close to his left ear Cinnamon murmured, "I sure am glad you made it safely, man."

He tried to sit up. Coming around the corner of the couch, she pushed him down again, a little further forward.

"My treat," she murmured. "Just relax."

It was like being in a dream. But it was a delightful dream. Eyes closed again, he felt his clothing being drawn aside and let it happen, like a co-operative patient obeying a nurse. His skin came alive, electrically, and from the recesses of his being energy flowed to concentrate at his groin.

"Ah!" Cinnamon whispered, and bestrode him. Astonished, disbelieving, he blinked long enough to see that her gaudy dress, top and bottom, had become a kind of girdle around her waist and she wore nothing else and her long arms, bare as her legs, were straight so her hands could clasp him at the base of his rib-cage while her spine curved and her face turned ceilingward and melted into a mirror of ecstasy while from contractions to convulsions the sheath she had put upon him carried his body with hers. It was over quickly, but it was flawless, and they cried in unison at the end.

Only then, shining-eyed, did she lean forward and lick his lips.

"Hey! You should get posted more often!" she said in a deep throaty voice. "How many times have I said leave the work to me tonight? How many times has your damned male machismo made you meddle when I needed it least?"

Concluding in a wave of laughter which made her internal muscles do delightful things: *"M-m-m-mmm . . . !* My *my!"*

Realization stabbed down Justin's spine like a spear of ice. For a second his spirit quailed at the implications; then he thrust her off him and forced himself upright, disregarding how ridiculous he must look with his pants around his ankles.

"Never!" he blurted, his voice a croak.

Caught off balance, halfway to anger, she snapped back, "What the hell you mean?"

Taking an enormous breath, he ploughed on doggedly. "Cinnamon, I've admired you for eight long years. All that time I've been more than half in love with you. But I never dared so much as put my arm around you. You frightened me! I thought—everybody thought—you were . . . Well, a repressed gay. *That's what I remember!"*

"Me, repressed?" she said automatically, with the air of one parrying a stale joke. But her reflex mockery died aborning. Slowly, as she digested what he had told her, her face changed.

She was almost grey when she managed to whisper, "Oh my God. You're not my Justin after all."

"That's right. And you're a different Cinnamon. Compared to what I remember, this has to be a different world."

EIGHT

I saw the entrance door
was made of mirror-glass
I saw my image in it
while reaching for the handle
I saw my reflection turn
and walk the other way

Even before he had finished speaking Justin felt cold. He clenched his fists as a shiver crawled down his back. Against his will, his teeth began to chatter; when he tried to lock them together, he failed. The room swam. For a moment he was afraid of throwing up, though luckily the surge of nausea passed as quickly as it had come on. He wanted to look at Cinnamon, but his neck-muscles also disobeyed him. His eyes were wide open, but they were focused on nothing in particular, and he felt that if he tried to move them the nausea would return.

Unable to look, he could however see, and at the edge of his field of vision saw her taking a deep breath, as to gather her forces for an enormous effort.

"Shock," he heard her murmur in a calm didactic tone as she thrust her dress down and stepped away from it, appearing in all her lean brown magnificence. Between her thighs light glinted on a trace of moisture from their coupling.

"Lie down," she said next, urging him to turn and comply with a tap on his shoulder. Then she stretched out alongside him and embraced him; there was terrifying strength in her arms and legs.

50

But it was comforting. Almost as though his body grew to realize it was futile to tremble against the restraint she had imposed, almost as though her warm breath on his face itself was enough to drive out the cold which had invaded him, he felt the surge of terror pass. It would recur; it must recur. But perhaps, if he was lucky, only in dreams.

For what had happened to him was suddenly obvious. At least he felt it was. It implied that posters could never safely be used for humans, but that was incidental. He said, "I'm better now. Thanks. Let me sit up."

Warily she did so. He re-arranged his clothing hastily.

"I've worked it out," he said. "What's happened must be like what made Gunther kill himself. Being posted must affect the mind. Obviously I've acquired false memories which . . ."

His voice trailed away as he realized she was slowly shaking her head.

"No?"

"No. Doesn't fit. I've been posted too, remember. Or is that one of the things you've forgotten?"

"Ah—no! I mean I remember that perfectly. Apart from the four military volunteers you were the first."

"*Military?*" she shot back.

"Oh my God." Justin put his head in his hands. "But I remember *that,* I swear I do! Who do you remember?"

She shrugged. "Four students from the science faculty."

"Impossible!" He sat bolt upright. "What about the security aspect?"

On the verge of making a retort, she checked.

"Man, you or I must be in trouble. Either way we need advice and help. I'm going to fix coffee and make a phone-call. You just wait a minute."

"Yeah. Yeah, okay." But his fingers were clenching over into his palms again. "Say, do you have a tranquillizer?"

"I do, but you don't get one. Maybe I shouldn't even give you coffee, just in case the poster did screw up your brain-chemistry . . . but it would have shown up in Herman's tests. I'll be right back."

Almost, seeing her turn away, he folded into a fetal ball. But at the back of his mind there was a hint of the fascination which had led him to the poster in the first place. (Once someone had told him, "Justin, you should have been a detective!" He cherished that remark as a compliment.) But it had been a long time —half eternity, it felt like!—since even a twinge of the same sensation had registered. Under the stifling régime of Chester and the DoD he had accomplished nothing new; the impulse to forge on, towards new discoveries, had been leached out of him.

Now, shockingly, he was faced with a puzzle even more involving. It aroused old faculties. He felt his imagination stirring from a long sleep, like the monster in the Yeats poem with its gaze "as blank and pitiless as the sun." He began to look on himself, on his predicament, as a riddle for the solving. Thus insulated from the feverish racking of his body, his mind grew clear. By the time Cinnamon, having donned a long red terry-cloth robe, brought mugs of steaming coffee he scarcely needed it.

"I called the restaurant," she said. "They were still there. Chester turned up after all, and they were having a last drink with him. They'll be here in a few minutes."

An electric jolt ran through him. "Hell! The last person I need to see right now!"

"Who—Chester?" She sat down on the next arm of the square U. "I don't understand . . . No, maybe I do. Justin, how do you think of the guy?"

His heart sank. That too, changed? But how could so many changes add up to so many things the same? His car, except for the untidiness which surprised him;

the people around him; the existence of Wright & Williams Inc. in the building he was familiar with!

Gruffly he said, "An ambitious bastard. Likes to buy people. Bought my soul, and yours. And if this is being recorded I don't care!"

"Yes, of course it is," she snapped. "After George Gunther's death—"

"He did at least kill himself?" Justin cut in.

"Sure he did! Though what a hell of a way to go— burning himself to death!"

Justin closed his eyes briefly. "He didn't shoot himself."

"No, of course—Oh, man!" She leaned forward and caught his hand. "No! He held the bag he was carrying up against his face, and when the thermite charge blew . . . Ugh!"

"We were talking," Justin said after a pause, "about Mr. T. Emory Chester. What's he like to you?"

"The greatest!" Cinnamon shook her head dolefully. "I don't know what else you can say about a guy who gives away two million a year, a million to underdeveloped countries and a million to pure research, and lives on a fraction of what he could be spending. Hell, there are accountants working for the Chester Foundation who take home more than he allows himself!"

In memory: Herman's voice talking about the man who financed the project . . .

"You mean it's still his money that's behind the poster? Not the Defense Department's? You said he was sweet-talking them—"

"Trying to keep their hands off us! They want to turn it into a military monopoly. That's why he's enlisted the support of the State Department and the Space Agency. Even he isn't rich enough to fund the entire development program."

That complete a shift in the situation was more than Justin's overloaded mind could cope with. He found himself literally gaping. Cinnamon started to laugh, doing her best to stifle it with the thick sleeve of her robe, but failing utterly. Abruptly he noticed there was a touch of hysteria in her mirth.

Of course! She too had been posted! And even if she denied that it had affected her . . .

It was his turn to offer comfort. Jumping up, he took the stride necessary to sit beside her and put his arm around her. Blindly she buried her face in his shoulder and for half a minute uttered great gasping sobs.

Apparently that was enough. An instant later, calm and composed, she was handing him his coffee and saying, "I have something to tell you about what *I* remember."

He nodded encouragement. Not looking at him, she went on, "When I first met you . . . No, that's wrong. For the whole of the first seven years I knew you, you scared me and I hated you as much as you seemed to hate me. You always gave the impression you were only tolerating me. You resented the fact that there had been someone else in the world working along the same lines as you. And then . . ." She took another deep breath.

"Then when I volunteered to be posted before you were it seemed to make a certain difference. It came across—listen, man, I *am* talking about the other Justin, you know?"

He shivered again, more violently. It was eerie to hear that said, but there was no way he could rebut it.

"It came across like you were being cowardly. You almost hoped something would go wrong, but knew what would happen if it did. So I did it, and when I arrived I was amazed. You hugged me! Then Levi put me through all those tests, and it took hours, and I was worn out, so you drove me home and came up here and—you didn't go home. I couldn't believe it! We wound up sitting here laughing at each other and saying why didn't we do it sooner? And it's gone on ever since."

"Less than perfect," Justin said.

After a fractional hesitation she nodded. "Yes. I can't help it. I'm a domineering sort of person. And I had the resentment to get rid of, piled up over seven long years, which I felt through being treated as an interloper."

She leaned forward earnestly. "But better than anything else I ever had! So I never said anything, except kind of as a joke, about the way he'd changed . . . Oh, Lord! It's getting to me. I'm sitting here talking to you, and I just said 'he'!"

"I like you a hell of a sight better than the Cinnamon I remember," Justin said. "But *where's the change?*"

There was a long thoughtful pause. Each of them was struggling with that mystery. Eventually there came the shrill cry of a door-bell.

"I guess they finally got here," Cinnamon sighed, stretching out her arm to tap a switch on the grey stone console. Briefly the television screen showed three faces, monstrously distorted by false perspective.

"Yes, there they are . . . Come in!" she added more loudly, and a concealed microphone picked up the order and released the lock. Turning to look at the new arrivals, Justin finally believed—in his guts, where it counted most—how different this world was that he had come to.

NINE

yes this is my street
the right distance along it
the right number on the gate
but whose car in the driveway
whose children on the lawn
whose wife puzzled at a stranger

Inarguably this was Chester—but transformed. Instead of being clean-shaven he sported a neat pointed beard, though no moustache. Instead of being formally clad to the point of dapperness, he wore an unpressed khaki suit with a safari-style belted jacket, its pockets full of pens and calculators and invisible lumpy objects, and a pair of open leather sandals over brown socks. He looked tired and irritable as he strode in and stared at Justin as though examining a specimen on a microscope slide.

Justin, speechless, stared back.

"He may not look any different," Cinnamon murmured at last, breaking the deadlock. "But he is. I promise you."

Suddenly Chester gave a harsh laugh. The effect was magical; all the suspicion and hostility in his face, which Justin would have recognized on the version he knew, was displaced by an expression of wry amusement.

"So what do we do—introduce ourselves?" he said. And suited action to word by offering his hand. Confused, Justin rose to take it, and thought to join in the joke.

"Glad to meet you, Mr. Chester," he muttered.

"What's with the 'mister' bit?" the millionaire countered. "Just plain Chester, as usual . . ." He hesitated, once more scrutinizing Justin. Finally he shook his head.

"I can't believe it, but if Cinnamon says it isn't the real you, I guess I can't challenge her. Who should know better? Honey, you got more of that coffee? I've had a long, long day. This on top of everything else I did not need!"

With the casualness of an old friend and regular visitor, he plumped himself down on the seating opposite Justin.

"I didn't tell Cinnamon your news on the phone," Levi said as he and Herman also sat down. "Figured you'd want to tell her yourself."

"That sounds alarming," Cinnamon said slowly. "Come on, Chester. What is it?"

Now, as fact piled on tiny fact, the reality of his predicament grew more and more acute in Justin's mind. For those few people who were allowed to address the Chester he knew informally, the style was always Emory, which had been his grandfather's first name.

He wondered whether there was a Zena di Cassio in this one's life, too . . .

Stretching, yawning, Chester said, "Almost the first use of the orbital poster is going to be the transfer of a human being back to Earth."

Levi and Herman gave lugubrious nods.

"But that's out of the question!" Cinnamon exclaimed. "After what happened to George, and now to Justin—and after what I'm afraid may have happened to me too—we can't risk it! What idiot made that decision?"

"No choice," Levi said. "You know they're trying to put an extension on Polly, the permanent orbital lab?"

"Of course!"

"One of the remote controls jammed on the new

section and the reaction motors didn't stop firing when they should have done. Dr. Landini got in the way of a half-ton girder. He has several broken ribs and a broken pelvis. He wouldn't live through a shuttle ride."

Before he could prevent himself Justin demanded, "Landini? Is that Ed Landini?"

They all glanced at him. Chester said, "Yes, I think his first name is Eduardo. Why?"

"The same one who was working on Project Ear?"

The instant he had uttered the words, Justin felt his heart sink. They wore uniformly blank expressions.

"There was never a Landini at Chester U," Cinnamon said at last. "Not in my time, anyhow."

"Nor mine," Chester said. "Honey, what about that coffee? I have this feeling we're into something incredibly important and my brain wants to take time out. Got any speed?"

"Speeds kills!" she retorted sharply. "Coffee's there—go help yourselves! This man is in trouble, hear?" She moved close to Justin and put her arm about his shoulders.

"What I can't understand"—his jaws were threatening to chatter again, but this time they were controllable, though it was hard talking through clenched teeth—"is how so many differences can add up to so much the same!"

"You'll have to explain that," Cinnamon encouraged. Thus reassured, Justin found the words come easier.

"In the world I remember, I was a partner in Wright & Williams Inc. It's the same here, right? The poster hall is on the top floor; the building is on the same site; maybe it looks a bit different on the outside but I wouldn't know because it was pretty well dark when we left it to go to the restaurant.

"But *my* version of Wright & Williams Inc. is financed by a Defense Department grant because the . . ." He hesitated, glancing sidelong at Chester, then gathered the courage to speak out.

"The T. Emory Chester I know is an ambitious politician who won't part with a cent of his own money, or the Foundation's, if he can avoid it. The State Department and the Space Agency only got to use the poster because they undertook to make their installations available on a priority basis to Army and Navy Intelligence."

While he was talking, Herman had gone quietly to the kitchen zone and brought mugfuls of coffee for his companions. Taking his with a word of thanks, Chester said, "But this is incredible! You're talking about the sort of person my family wanted me to turn into. But you look like the Justin I know—you sound like him, except that maybe you're a bit more diffident . . . Hell, how can I take this seriously? So many differences *must* make a different world, whether it's a real one or an illusory one! They *can't* add up to the same!"

"My point exactly!" Justin riposted, leaning forward. "Tell me this. Do you know somebody called Zena di Cassio?"

There was an instant of frigid silence. At some point Cinnamon had countermanded the music; all that could be heard was the hum of the electronics and a distant murmur of late-night traffic.

Suddenly, although the air of the room was at a comfortable temperature, sweat glistened visibly on Chester's face. His features set in a rigid mask as he stared at Justin, seeming to want to penetrate the other man's face and see into his very mind.

Stirring at last, deliberately turning aside and placing his coffee-mug on the handier of the black-topped tables, he spoke in a voice that revealed how much effort he was investing in self-control. It was totally unlike the way he had been talking before: slow, tense, trembling on the verge of fury.

"If you think knowing that name will do you any good, you better think again! Tell me who mentioned it!"

The others looked on in total astonishment. It was plain, Justin saw from their expressions, that they had no idea why Chester was reacting in this fashion. Oblivious of the impact he was making, he rushed on.

"Was it her? Personally? If you know where she is, tell me! I'd like to tear her limb from limb!"

Abruptly he grew aware of the way his listeners were staring at him. He paled, licking his lips, doubling his hands into fists, fighting something within himself . . . and winning. A few seconds passed, and he jumped to his feet and walked a few paces across the floor. With his back turned, he said, "I don't understand how you could have heard about her. I don't understand!"

Cinnamon looked an appeal at Justin; Levi and Herman seemed completely baffled.

"In the world I remember," Justin said reluctantly, "T. Emory Chester lives with her . . . Oh, God! I don't know whether to say *lives* or *lived!*"

"I think," Cinnamon said with cautious firmness, "you'd better explain this, Chester."

Still with his back to them, breathing heavily, he began to relax. Turning around, not looking directly at them, he said, "Okay. I never told anybody before, and I'm afraid of telling you now. But . . . Oh, what the *hell?* I guess I may have earned the right to live down my past."

"When I asked Cinnamon this evening what she thought of you," Justin said, "she told me you're the greatest. She actually said—no, don't interrupt, Cinnamon!—there's no other way to describe someone who gives away two million a year and lives on a fraction of what he could spend."

"Thank you," Chester said, closing his eyes briefly. "That was what I needed to hear. I guess I do have the guts to talk about it after all. And—and heaven only knows where you could have found out about her . . . Do you swear you're telling the truth?"

"Yes. Without reservation." Sensing it was necessary, Justin spoke in a formal, solemn tone.

"Okay, then." Chester resumed his seat; he was still sweating enormously. "I did once know a woman called Zena di Cassio. How she latched on to me, I never dared ask. But when I was still pretty much a kid—twenty-two, twenty-three—she turned up in my life. I'd just about realized . . ."

He hesitated, glancing from one to other of them. Reading no more than sympathetic interest in their faces, he took the plunge.

"I'd just about realized that because of the way I was brought up—you know the standard deprived-rich-kid syndrome, 'my son the status symbol', all that kind of shit!—I was never going to have much of a sex-life except under . . . Christ, it's hard to find the words! Maybe I should have acquired a shrink the way most people do if their parents show no interest in them, but I always hated that idea . . . Let's say: under exceptional conditions.

"Arrives Zena."

He was speaking in a more natural fashion now, as though the mere utterance made for a catharsis.

"She understood people like me, fixated on stern European nannies and governesses—oh, my family had the whole gamut of that! She also understood perfectly how to manipulate kids like me in order to get control of their money. The six months after she turned up in my life were almost the happiest I ever spent. Would have been, except that they were also the most miserable. I could feel myself being bribed into plastic. I wasn't going to be myself any more when I reached the point of total dependence—of addiction? Yes, that's the word. Do you want all the filthy details? All the smut?" He glared about him defiantly.

Cinnamon said, "You don't have to make it any clearer. We understand you wanted to be punished for what wasn't your fault."

He nodded grimly. "But it wasn't just the whipping bit. It was the whole complex of it. I knew what I ought to do with the fortune I'd inherited, but I was scared of cutting loose and doing something on my own. I wanted my life to go on being run by someone else, someone in authority over me, who would grant me a bit of sex now and then as a reward, the kind of affection I never had when I was a child. And so on. Oh, I guess I'm a classic case!

"And then a miracle happened." He was very much calmer now, and the sweat no longer shone on his skin. "I won't bore you with the details, but I found the guts to come out and admit I was gay and with a man I didn't need all the trimmings I did—do—with a woman. So I took the best decision of my life and told that bitch to go dig herself a grave and lie down in it. What became of her, I've no idea. I only know that I've never hated anybody in my life so much as I hated her the day I realized what it was she had set out to do to me."

He turned burning eyes on Justin.

"And what was my situation in the world you claim to remember?"

Justin described it, phrasing it as gently as he could, but making Chester tremble from head to toe.

"Oh my God," he said at last. "That's terrible! It's so exactly the way I was sure I must turn out if I let her go on running my life . . ."

He pulled out a handkerchief and wiped his forehead.

"I believe you," he said suddenly. "I don't understand how it could possibly happen, but—yes, okay! You are another Justin than the person I remember."

"And I'm another Cinnamon." She spoke in a clear level voice, but the hands in which she cradled her empty coffee-mug shook just a little. She summarized what she had earlier told Justin.

"You never mentioned that before!" Levi said accusingly.

"Why should I? The changes in the world I found after being posted were tiny, and all for the better." She bit her lower lip. "Now I think back, I do recall that for the next few weeks I kept forgetting where I'd put things, finding them in unexpected places. I came across a couple of books I didn't know I had, and some other things too—ornaments, a pair of shoes . . . But I only thought hell! I'm getting old before my time! I'm suffering from absent-mindedness!"

"Did none of your volunteers mention anything like that?" Justin demanded of Levi. "I guess you followed them up?"

"Well, sure! But . . . No, I never investigated that aspect."

"Why should you?" Justin said, hunching forward. "You had no reason to imagine that being posted would change somebody—or maybe that isn't right. Maybe it's the world that's changed, not the person." He scowled into nowhere. "I can't figure out how, and I'm not even sure if what I just said makes sense. It can't be that operating a poster creates a field which alters the world! Otherwise all our tests with inanimate objects and electronic equipment would have done so."

"Maybe they did," Herman said after a pause.

"Save it," Levi said tiredly. "For all we know the world was created one second ago, your memories and mine included—right?"

"And solipsism is the only ultimately defensible philosophical standpoint," Cinnamon snapped. "Don't waste breath on logic-chopping! But there's one important point you've overlooked."

"What?"—in chorus.

"The longer the trip, the more radical the difference. I was posted about a kilometer, like the student volunteers—whom Justin remembered as military, by the way."

"Tell you about that later," Justin said. "Go on, Cinnamon!"

"And I've told you what difference I found on arrival. Negligible. As for the change in me—Chester?"

Reverting completely to normal, as though his confession had been traumatic but its reception perfectly restorative, Chester said promptly, "For the better, honey. All of it."

"You did notice a change?" she persisted.

"No more than could be accounted for by doing something you felt proud of. I've been through that. I just told you."

She gave him a flashing smile, and continued.

"But George Gunther was posted to Eastern Europe. And on arrival he was obviously insane. Right?"

"I think I see what you're getting at," Justin said slowly. "So could I have been, except I came the other way . . . Say! Is there a Project Touchstone in this world?"

Chester and Levi looked blank. Unexpectedly Herman spoke up.

"Yes, it's a Navy project. Communication with nuclear-armed submarines, prevent them firing without full authority. They say it works fine."

"Why do you ask?" Cinnamon said.

"In my world"—it was amazing how easily the phrase came to his tongue—"it was the project to put posters in all our overseas embassies. Which brings me back to my main point.

"How the hell can so many differences add up to so much same?"

TEN

here is what you'll need
they said when he set out
passport guidebook foreign money
but the passport held no visa
the guidebook had blank pages
and the money turned out to be forged

There was a pause. Cinnamon broke it, rising to her feet.

"It's no use speculating," she said firmly. "We've got to take a look at the basics of the problem."

She strode across the room to her computer terminal, kicked around a chair, and picked up an enormous pair of glasses, which she slipped on. The others were making to follow her; she checked them with a wave.

"I can dupe this for you on the TV," she said over her shoulder as her fingers ran light across the keys. "Stay where you are and be comfortable."

A standard comm mode layout sprang up on both screens with a HELLOP heading and a request for identification. She logged in, waited a moment to be recognized, and then requested access to the main poster file.

"You interrogate your main program in comm mode?" Justin said incredulously.

65

"Oh, we're very informal at Chester," answered Cinnamon without looking round, as though explaining to a stranger. She caught herself and now did glance at him.

"Why do you ask? Did you do it differently?"

"We sure did!" Rising, he went to look over her shoulder. "I wouldn't even have been allowed to admit over my home terminal that such a program existed! Let alone wire into it. I can see I have a hell of a lot to re-learn."

"Well, I kind of like my programs to be on friendly terms with me," Cinnamon murmured, hitting a double CRLF and leaning back in her chair.

SEC said the screens, and then abruptly there was the title-page of the poster program. Justin scanned it eagerly.

"That's different!" he exclaimed, pointing. "And that! And—My God, if that means what I think it means, we never got into that area at all! Say, don't JeRST yet!"—as Cinnamon wiped the display.

"I want to find out," she said curtly, "whether distance travelled has anything to do with magnifying the effect."

"If it does," Chester said around a yawn, "you'd better find out before they post Landini back from orbit. Not that I can see any reasonable alternative if a shuttle flight would kill him."

"Where is the Polly right now?" Levi demanded.

"Where it always is," Herman supplied. "Circular orbit at about five hundred klick."

"Then that's much less distance than Justin was posted over. If by any miracle the effect is exponential with increasing distance, say a power-relationship—"

"Can it!" Cinnamon snapped. The screens showed the basic poster equations.

"What's that?" Levi asked.

"Levi, I don't have time to explain! Shut up!" She

ran forward to the first-, second-, third-, fourth-, eventually fifth-order derivatives, that being the level where macro effects started to be discernible. Forgetting his own plight, forgetting there were other people present, Justin watched in fascination.

"I think I follow that, but we discarded your notation. It was a crock and kept on biting bags."

"Didn't it generate a demon after it had been running a while? Ours did, bless its little cotton socks . . . There!" Her tone mixing dismay with satisfaction, Cinnamon ran her cursor along the bottom line of the current display.

"What's that?" Levi called.

"It's a factor specifying congruity between dispatch and destination posters. But I just realized what it doesn't specify. Justin, are you with me?"

He straightened suddenly; he had been leaning on the back of her chair.

"Oh, Christ," he said softly, his face paling in the low light. "It doesn't specify congruency between the universes of the two posters."

"That's right," Cinnamon said with a sober nod. "If there are posters in operation in an infinite number of universes, the chance necessarily exists that one or—what am I *saying?*—an infinite number of them must be more congruent to the dispatch poster than the one you intended the consignment to go to."

Chester, sitting upright and staring, was making heavy weather of this. Herman and Levi were doing little better, but Levi ventured, "Are you talking about parallel worlds?"

"I guess I am," Cinnamon said wearily, passing her hand across her forehead. "Never thought of it before, but it fits, doesn't it? What I've been through, what Justin's been through . . . It wasn't the George Gunther we knew who killed himself. It was someone from another and much more paranoid version of reality."

They sat stunned for a few seconds. Then Herman erupted, "Now just a moment, Cinnamon! Before you start fantasizing, what about the other alternatives?"

"Are there any?"

"Well—well, sure there are!" Herman groped in the air, as though hoping a miracle would put the explanation into his hand. "Suppose the posting process alters people's perception of reality! Then—"

"Won't work," Justin cut in. "Try and figure the odds against a consistent distortion occurring."

"How do I know one has?" Levi said swiftly, taking up Herman's point. "So far, and it's only been a matter of a few hours, what we've learned about 'your world' strikes me as thoroughly inconsistent! Apparently I exist there, like Chester and Herman and Cinnamon, *and* you drive the same kind of car *and* Wright & Williams Inc. is in the same place *and*—and so on!" He threw up his hands. "You said it yourself: so many differents can't make a same!"

"That isn't what he said," Chester objected. "He was asking *how* they could."

"It's impossible," Herman snapped, and sat back with his arms folded.

Alarmed, Justin took a step towards him.

"Are you implying I'm deranged? That what I've been through has turned my mind?"

"I don't know what's happened to you," Herman said sullenly. "But whatever it is, it can't possibly be that you've been shifted from one universe to another."

"Herman, there's nothing wrong with Justin which showed up in my tests," Levi interposed. "I don't believe he suddenly went off his head."

"You believe these far-fetched claims, then?"

"I—I guess I don't have enough evidence to make up my mind yet."

"Then you better get some, and make it fast!"

Levi said in a meant-to-be-soothing voice, "There

were a good few non-living consignments, weren't there? And all of them got through safely, right?"

"Bar one garbled code-group," Justin said unthinkingly. And flushed to realize they were suddenly staring at him.

"What code-group?" Cinnamon said at length.

"I—uh—I don't know exactly, but I remember a complaint from the embassy . . ." His words trailed away and he concluded with a shrug. "Guess that's another thing that happened in my world and not in yours, then."

"But . . ." Levi, in turn, was grasping at the air. "But even if your hypothesis is correct, Cinnamon, and it seems pretty flimsy, where does the change arise? Do your equations tell you that?" He pointed at the TV screen.

"Yes," was her prompt and disconcerting reply, and she flicked back to the title-page of the program before singling out a dense array of symbology that overfilled the screen and automagically appeared as a rolling display.

"That," she went on, "is the specification-set for a basic rho-space environment. Most of it is fudge, of course—you can't think in rho-space terms if you live in normal space—but look here." She spotted her cursor and set it to fidgeting back and forth under a group of eight or nine symbols.

"Justin, you read that?"

"I'm afraid I do," Justin muttered with reluctance. "It implies that there can't be *a* rho-space. There must be an infinite number of them. My God, how did I come to miss that?" He clapped his palms to his temples.

"If it's any comfort, so did I, and so did the other you," Cinnamon sighed. "An infinite number of us did, I guess . . . Say!" She brightened suddenly. "I wonder what they're doing, the ones who got it right!"

"Cinnamon, that's way down on the puddle," Justin reproved her sharply.

"No, it's crucial!" she retorted, swinging to face him. "It can't possibly follow that the operation of a poster creates a rho-space. It can only invoke it. A quick approximation ought to tell us"—she reverted to the terminal—"whether there's a limit to the number of rho-spaces a particular operation can invoke, or . . . Jesus Christ, look at that!"

The screen was suddenly full of 1's and the display was rolling.

"It's too quick!" Justin objected. "It must still be searching—"

"I don't know how your sandpipers were rated but we have a deal of picosecond gear in there now!" Cinnamon rapped. "That's a genuine readout! It'll never stop!"

"But that means—" Justin began. The sound of a phone interrupted him. The nearest receiver was beside Cinnamon; she seized it, listened, thrust it towards Chester.

"For you, and it's a grand panic!"

He jumped up and took the phone aside, speaking with his hand cupped around the mouthpiece. Disregarding him, Justin carried on determinedly.

"That means every poster program must contain not merely demons but daemons, built into the actual machinery, and they don't search for what we want to be transferred. They simply take the nearest—"

"The nearest congruent item," Cinnamon finished for him. "That is, the nearest in a rho-space direction. Not in the universe of departure."

While they were still trying to digest the implications of that, Chester said to the phone, "Sure, I'll get them there right away."

And, turning to look at them all with a face like his own death-mask, said, "They had to rush the job of posting Dr. Landini back from orbit. He was going to die of his internal hemorrhages. So they did one quick dry run with a chunk of equipment, and it worked, so they sent him.

"But what arrived in the delivery poster wasn't Landini.

"It isn't even a human being."

ELEVEN

two sleeping-pills as always
bringing guaranteed oblivion
in the night a whirlwind
by day a cold awakening
in a room full of wreckage
with only the sky for a ceiling

The Chester whom Justin remembered owned an executive jet. This one had an elderly compact car and two bicycles. It was an Air Force plane which rushed them to the isolated site in Central Texas where the Space Agency had built its poster evaluation facility.

So many things different, yet so many the same! Justin tried to wrestle with the problem again during the flight, but exhaustion claimed him. In any case it was too huge a mystery to unravel all at once. First he must get to grips with the ways in which what he found here differed from what he had been used to.

Some points were coming clear already, at least by implication. Here were the same crises: dwindling resources, pollution, a battle between vested economic interests and those who dreamed of a more stable, less wasteful civilization. However, the official paranoia he was accustomed to was far less acute. Instead of treating the situation as though it were the result of enemy action, drafting blanket legislation of a type previously seen only during a war—which, Justin had often sourly thought, was largely intended to ensure that as many citizens as possible could legally be entered in Federal computer-files—people in this world were relying more on self-help and local disbursement of national funds.

The system obviously had its faults; above all, the establishment of solar power satellites remained what it would have been in his old world, a mere technological fix and not a long-term solution.

But on the way to the airport nearest Chester U he noticed, parked in the dark and empty streets, a number of pieces of "Detroit iron" on whose doors were boldly-painted numerals: 22.6, 23.1, 21.9 . . .

Curious enough to ask Cinnamon what they were, he learned that these cars' owners had modified them to save fuel. Under a government scheme they could obtain a certificate showing that by test they had converted a vehicle which used to burn a gallon in twelve or fourteen miles so that now it achieved over twenty. There was a legendary fixer, she said with a wry smile, who had exceeded fifty on a car which originally managed fifteen. But he was invariably in some other state.

"You've always known about that, haven't you?" Justin asked after a pause to reflect on how much better this approach was than the sledgehammer techniques he had experienced.

"You mean from before I was posted?"

"Yes."

She nodded. "But come to think of it, of course, it may not operate here just the way I described. Oh, man!" She caught his hand impulsively. "I feel like you pulled the Earth out from under me!"

"I did," Justin said roughly, freeing himself and turning away, to go on staring at the night-time city where every corner revealed another change from what he recollected. "But at least there's no more room for argument about that."

By now the world about him felt as fragile as tissue-paper.

It was dawn when their plane landed on the Texas strip. Scores of people, a few in uniform, most in civilian garb, rushed to meet it. At their head was a plump dark middle-aged woman whom both Justin and Cinnamon recognized—but whose name here was Dr. Inez Martí. Justin had known her as Dr. Hamilton, her married name. And the other Dr. Hamilton was here, Eustace Hamilton who had come to Chester U in the early days of the poster project, who had given a glowing report to the Space Agency, setting all this scheme in motion . . .

How in all the infinite universe *could* there be so many differences when this entire site looked just as he remembered, down to most of the staff? He was mechanically saying, between yawning and rubbing his red-rimmed eyes, hello and how are you? The sole new arrival who was a stranger was Herman, but Levi was recognized, Chester, Cinnamon of course . . .

Useless to try and keep track. Let it happen, blame his *faux pas* on fatigue. It was the only sensible course.

"Under the circumstances it was imperative to get Ed Landini back to an Earthside hospital," Inez Martí said. She stood at the end of a long conference table which had individual computer terminals at each place. Behind her a wall-hung display screen copied in two-meter size what was showing on the miniature screens elsewhere. "But even the relatively gentle g-force of the shuttle, if you applied it to a rib-cage in that condition—"

"Inez!" said Eustace Hamilton in a tone which convinced Justin that, although she used her old name, these two must be married in this world as well. "We don't need any more justification. We only need to figure out what the hell has happened to Ed—and what it is we've got instead."

"Hear hear!" came a loud chorus. Everybody at the table looked as though he or she had been roused from sleep prematurely, or stayed up long past the end of a regular tour.

"Pictures!" someone said.

Inez shrugged and tapped a code into the terminal before her. And there it was: full-color, sharp definition—and ungraspable.

Justin stared for a long moment before realizing that he was, despite information received, trying to make a human out of this creature. Perspective foreshortened it; it was lying on a stretcher with two baffled-looking white-coated nursing orderlies standing beside it.

"Inez, that's not much use," Justin called. "Give us a rotatory transform into an upright posture if you haven't taken any full-length shots."

Several people nodded surprised approval. Sighing, Inez gave the necessary instruction.

"If you'll be patient, we'll have a direct line to the hospital ward where it's being cared for," she muttered. "I was told it could be patched in before you got here, but . . . That do?"

Abruptly the creature was something that might have evolved on Earth, and hadn't. For a second Justin thought it was canine, but that was preconception at work again. It was a biped, it was bibrachial, it had much larger hindquarters than a human and its thorax, though deep, was improbably narrow—but there were reasons for that not being quite accurate, chief of which was that it wore a yellow spacesuit. And *that* could have been manufactured, if not in the States, then perhaps in one of the countries lately launching its own space-program, like China or one of the Arab nations. It was recognizable as what it was.

But it lacked the helmet. And the creature's head, tilted to one side and with the mouth open, was the most shocking and also the most fascinating thing on the screen.

It had a high-domed skull. It had ears set low at the back; only one, of course, was visible, but it could be seen that its pinna was an erectile flap. It had a snout like a baboon's . . . but not quite. For the reason Justin had thought "canine" was that more than anything else this head resembled a clean-shaven—no, somewhat stubble-cheeked—boxer dog. Not snout. *Muzzle.* And the folded skin, on forehead and jaw, somewhat pinkish, quite conventional in shade, but the nose blunt and marked by a darker zone, a sort of areola, roughly heart-shaped, and the eyes behind it deeply sunken, protected by enormous brow-ridges or possibly cartilaginous pads . . .

For a second Justin felt a surge of overwhelming joy. If it were only true—God, let it be true!—that because of what he had done humanity was at last to be put in touch with fellow intelligences wearing different bodily shapes—! What a climax for one person's lifetime of endeavor! What a fulfillment of all his half-formed ambitions! Project Ear was nothing compared to this miracle!

And then someone, a woman rising at the back of the hall, framed the all-important question.

"Elaine Rotblat, medical!" she identified herself. "Inez, is it going to survive?"

"Maybe," was the grim reply. "It's still unconscious. It must be pretty badly injured. It arrived strapped to a prosthetic support, see?" She ran a cursor across the screen.

Dr. Rotblat whistled loudly. "Well, I'll be . . . If that's to protect the site of injuries . . ."

All eyes turned on her; she was a small, pale woman with untidy fair hair, staring at the screen through heavy glasses.

"What?" said Eustace impatiently.

"Don't you see?" she exclaimed, pointing. "Broken ribs! Broken pelvis! Just the kind of injuries they said Ed Landini had sustained!"

There was a brief silence, broken by the intrusion of an anonymous voice.

"Inez, for Chrissake clear down those screens! We

want to pipe you the alien in real time and you've wedged every damned input channel!"

"Oh, shit," Inez muttered. "*I* didn't know putting on a rotatory transform wedged anything! Get someone to slop that—we'll be needing the facility a lot. Clearing now. Okay?"

The screens all blanked.

"With you semi-immediately," the voice said, and cut off. Lights which had automatically been dimmed while the wall-display was in use came up to normal level.

A shiver crawled down Justin's spine. For the first time he had heard the term "alien" used in the sense he recollected from his boyhood reading of science fiction.

And the same instant brought a realization which up to now had been concealed from him by fatigue. These people were being so matter-of-fact, it was incredible! What he sensed around him was excitement, not terror; this was perhaps the greatest single event in human history, but no one was overwhelmed by it. Whereas the world he recollected from "before," one might say, was set up to exclude the possibility of aliens . . . or even of foreigners.

Tantalizingly, a possible clue to his predicament hovered at the edge of his mind; elusive as a dream, it faded when he saw a picture of the alien suitless and on a hospital bed. Simultaneously a running commentary was heard, already in progress.

"—unconscious and very weak, but has a regular pulse about seventy to the minute and is breathing shallowly about four or five to the minute. He's obviously male. His blood is red and we've sent it to be typed though we don't expect to be able to give a transfusion, of course. Sonic probes of his torso indicate a typical mammalian skeleton with ribs and pelvis, and so far as we've yet determined the internal organs correspond to ours, even though the match is poor. What?"

—in answer to an unheard question. "Oh, we took a blood-sample with a sterile lance for culture purposes. He looks enough like us for there to be a risk of cross-infection. Also we want to know whether we can safely give him nourishment, like sugar-syrup or something else basic. He could be levo for all we can tell by just looking, same as us, or he might equally be dextro and metabolically incompatible. In which case we'll have some real hard programs to hack—"

Someone turned the commentary down, and the lights, which once again had dimmed the moment the pictures came on, grew bright as before. Blinking, annoyed, they all turned to look towards the door. Standing at the foot of the table was a brown-haired man whom Justin recognized with sinking heart.

"Lieutenant-General Lane!" he identified himself in a harsh tone. "I'm told the inventors of the poster are here, Dr. Williams and Dr. Wright."

Glancing at Cinnamon, Justin shrugged when she showed no sign of recognizing Lane. They both rose.

"Ah!" Lane continued with heavy irony. "We have a few questions to put to you. Specifically, how the hell a monster came to be in the poster instead of Ed Landini! Dr. Martí"—more sharply and more loudly. "Next time a VIP comes in, check with the dragon before you kidnap him. These people will be a sight more useful where I'm taking them!"

TWELVE

no sweat a wolf can be tamed
you just imprint him as a cub
bet he'll remember me—you watch
hi boy I fed you from a bottle
but christ the hormonal revolution
now dirk the teeth now blade the claws

And abruptly this world was much more like the one Justin remembered.

He and Cinnamon had been whisked to an improvised facility conjured up specifically because what had been posted from orbit was a problem; hence the faulty computer links. Preparations had been made to receive and treat Landini, and they were being adapted on the spur of the moment. Those involved had taken it for granted that nothing could possibly be more important than keeping the alien alive and—given that if it wore a spacesuit it must be intelligent—communicating with it . . . unless, of course, it were a test animal.

But there were other people, who had taken rather longer to arrive on the scene, whose primary concern was with the Polly—the Permanent Orbital Laboratory—and its crew. The poster terminal was here; the shuttle landing-ground was where it had always been in Justin's experience, to the north, in desert country; its communications set-up had been doubled to this site in case of a crash which would not only disable the shuttle facility but also wipe irreplaceable computer records. The place to which Cinnamon and Justin were now taken, therefore, was a concrete bunker smelling of stagnant air where a dozen tired-faced men and women were firing up standby equipment and discovering case after case of software rot as they tried to lock into the main circuits.

Also there were an admiral and a man with the indefinable aura of a career civil service officer. Justin wished fervently that Chester—in either of the versions known to him—could be here, but he had been denied permission to accompany them, and was still arguing.

As soon as they were marched in, Cinnamon boiled over.

"What the hell is the point of bringing us here?" she exploded, looking over the rows of consoles, chairs, screens, and keyboards which identified the bunker for what it was. "You could at least have taken us to the faulty poster!"

That was a mistake. Too late Justin tried to interrupt. Almost purring, the admiral advanced.

"You're Dr. Wright? I'm Admiral Laura Clancy. I'm glad to hear you admit that your poster is at fault."

Making a gallant recovery, Cinnamon said, "If something goes in one end and something else comes out the other, of course there must be a fault."

"It seems logical," murmured the man in plain clothes, advancing towards them. "I'm Geary S. Fowler, in case you'd forgotten. Good to see you both again."

Justin, in a momentary fit of panic, glanced at Cinnamon, but she was looking as blank as he felt. Fowler came to the rescue.

"We met only once, in Washington, when you came to lobby us along with Mr. Chester in search of funds. I voted for you. You can imagine how embarrassing my situation is right now, I'm sure, or will be next time I attend a meeting of the Appropriations Committee. That is, unless we find a way out of this *impasse*."

There was a pause. Lane stepped into the breach.

"Geary, we need some clear explanations—right now!" he declared. "I was given to understand that this poster was infallible. Now it turns out it scrambles people!"

"Scrambles?" Cinnamon repeated incredulously. "My God, you make it sound like one of those imaginary gadgets in a thirties magazine, that scans you and transmits a radio signal to be converted back to matter at the other end."

Justin had been about to say much the same, but—as ever—had been less quick than his partner to put ideas into words. Now he hastened to her support.

"Are you implying that you think this—this *alien* with the same kind of injuries as Landini . . . *is* Landini?"

Cinnamon's face lit up, eyes and mouth rounding into O's. She made the same shape at him with thumb and forefinger. A hit, a palpable hit!

"I don't know what to think!" the general roared. "Nor do the crew of the Polly! And that's what I'm worried about. One moment they were congratulating themselves on getting their colleague back to Earth alive, and the next, they were being rewarded with dead silence apart from routine machine communications. We're having to keep them in ignorance of what's happened. Out on a space-station people become very interdependent, you know. It's the isolation. If we have to explain that Landini didn't make it . . ."

He concluded with a shrug and turned away. Suddenly Justin badly needed to know who this version of him was. He leaned close to Cinnamon.

"Have you met him before? No? But heard of him?"

"Of course!" She raised her eyebrows as she answered in an equally soft tone. "Oldest man who ever got assigned to a lunar mission . . . Oh. Not in your world?"

Miserably Justin shook his head. He felt as though the stars in the sky were leaning on him, making him over into a twentieth-century Atlas who must hold up the heavens at all costs, and he was condemned to be crippled at every turn.

More and more the knowledge was coming real to him that a poster must be the key to an infinity of universes, and along with that awareness went the sober recognition that human beings are very finite creatures indeed.

Cinnamon, gathering her forces, said briskly, "Well, we'd better begin at the beginning, I guess." Striding forward, she cast an expert eye over the facilities which the staff were firing up. "Hmm! Half this stuff is five years old and some is more like seven, but I guess if you can make it work it may do. Where's the monitor to connect us with the Polly?"

She put the question at random to a young man in white overalls, busy checking circuitry with a hand-held readout board. His answer was a curt word: "Any!"

"That's a fair start," Cinnamon continued, unfazed. "And can you patch me into the Chester University computers from here?"

"What? Oh!" The young man looked up. "I guess so, but it may take some hairy interfacing. There's a lot of stuff at Chester that isn't integrated yet . . . Say, are you from there? Isn't that where they designed the poster?"

The word spread rapidly around the dismal room, and several of the staff broke off what they were doing and converged towards Cinnamon, their expressions anxious. Lane roused himself and likewise approached.

"Okay! So what do you think should be done?" he demanded.

"First off, tell the crew of the Polly that—" Cinnamon hesitated fractionally, reviewing her terminology. "That *the casualty* survived transfer and is being treated. Give it a gloss of verisimilitude by describing the operation needed to repair broken ribs. Or something like that. I'm no expert in fudge-factors! But fudge the situation somehow along those lines. Then get back to

normal as best you can. Keep their heads occupied with
the minutiae of the job—have they rectified this, have
they sorted out the other? Oh, for Chrissake! Why do
I have to tell you how to treat it like an Apollo 13?"

Lane had been about to snap at her. He visibly
changed his mind. Giving a grim nod, he turned away
and began to issue orders.

"We can patch you into Chester U," said the young
man in white, who had rapidly interrogated a nearby
terminal. "It may take a while before the interfacing is
fully established, but if you'd like to tell me what file to
shoot for . . ."

"Just give me a board," Cinnamon said, dropping
into a nearby chair. "And one for Justin too. And don't
forget to cut us out of comm mode with anything that's
being piped to orbit!"

"Of course not," the young man said in an injured
tone, and sat down to compile the requisite patchwork.

Waiting for something familiar, or at least analyzable,
to crop up on the screen assigned to him, Justin mar-
velled yet again at the incredibly close correspondence
between this world and his old one. He had ceased
already to think of it as "his own"—the chance of getting back to it, even had he wanted to, was of the order
of reciprocal ∞.

Must be. He didn't need a computer to help him
check *that* calculation.

But the likenesses were so much more amazing than
the differences! Given the assumption that something—
for instance, an act of free will—might alter the frame-
work of "reality," and that the consequences of every
such act were "real" in their own separate ways, then
why was this world so astonishingly close to his own,
populated by people he recognized, speaking English,
owning the same kind of things, acting in the same
sort of way? Were there nodes and nexuses? Were there
levels on which certain decisions acted to cancel others
made at a lower level? If so how? Surely the corollary

of accepting the notion of free will as a determining factor meant that every act of will must be borne out in practice: from *yes* to *no* via a literally countless series of *maybe*.

He felt dizzy as he contemplated the implications. He was at once Descartes, trying to reconcile the immaterial with its material vehicle, and Plato, trying to transcend both in search of the ideal. As soon as his imagination turned outward, towards the infinity of stars, of galaxies, of island universes, he felt something inside him quail, as though he were looking at himself through the wrong end of a microscope, and everything he had ever respected about himself, as being substantial, were fading to insignificance.

Yet his instinct rebelled. He was still aware of his physical envelope; he still had eyes and hands and legs and a brain to reason with, against no matter what odds. And he still had genitals, symbolic of some kind of triumph against entropy. He felt them stir as he glanced admiringly at Cinnamon, envying her capacity to cope but remembering that she had come less far to this strange world, and was better acquainted with it, and . . .

And suddenly was terrified of being trapped in infinite regress. Given *this* has changed, then it follows *that* has changed, and at every subsequent level—just like a demon working down a computer program—there are consequent changes. Every individual difference is multiplied appallingly, as in a hall of mirrors to the nth!

Yet it wasn't working out that simply. And what did the poster have to do with it? Did ultra-logical machinery—?

The train of thought was fragmented by a signal coming up in URGENT URGENT mode on all screens not already pre-empted. The interior of the bunker looked like a lunatic Christmas tree, flashing and flashing.

CHESTER TO JUSTIN AND CINNAMON SCREAMER SCREAMER

"I'll be damned," Cinnamon said softly. "Trust that cat to break loose before you or I can make it!"

ALIEN IS RECOVERING

ALIEN IS LEVO LIKE US

ALIEN APPEARS TO BE HUMAN AT LEAST COMPUTANALYSIS SHOWS 46 CHROMOSOMES AND AS YET HAS NOT DIFFERENTIATED DOWN TO DISCRIMINATORY LEVEL SO MUST BE LOW MOLECULAR SCREAMER

"Human?" Lane said disbelievingly. But the resonance of the statement had transfixed Justin, even before the full version appeared. This time the implications were genuinely terrifying: that one could take a—a *stranger* like the one he had seen stretched on a hospital bed, and cross it with a familiar person (Cinnamon?) and beget maybe something like the offspring of a horse and a donkey, in other words a mule.

It was only a logical extension of what he already knew to be the truth. But it was too much. He moaned and fell forward, clutching his head in his hands.

THIRTEEN

suppose you dreamed
of being in an unknown country
its language incomprehensible
it writing indecipherable
without recollection of going there
and waking found it was for instance Korea

"Justin! Justin, wake up!"

He was awake—had been for some while—only he hadn't yet opened his yes. An insight had come to him during the long hours he had spent sleeping, and he was desperate not to let it slip away.

Now, however, he felt he had it safely in his grasp. He could risk being roused. He was in a hospital bed. Cinnamon, her face concerned, was leaning over him; behind her were Chester and Herman, and beyond them a nurse and a young doctor he didn't recognize. Intending to say hello, he was caught out by a huge yawn which turned into a chuckle. He sat up.

"You had to have a sedative," Cinnamon explained. "It was the aftermath of the shock you hadn't yet digested."

"That figures. Where am I?"

"In the base infirmary."

"How long have I been out?"

"More than a day."

That shook Justin. "What about the alien?" he demanded after a moment.

"They decided to take the risk of operating while he was still unconscious," Herman said, stepping nearer.

Justin whistled. "How did it go?"

"Incredibly well. The surgeon says he's like a computer transform of a human. They didn't dare transfuse him with anything but neutral saline, of course, but they managed to keep up his body-fluid level, and a fast computer run-down on his liver secretions showed that he metabolizes glucose, same as we do, so at least they've been able to pump some nourishment into him. He'll be weak when he wakes up—"

"Did they give him a human-type anaesthetic?" Justin cut in.

"They hoped to get the whole job done before he recovered from whatever sedation he was already under," Herman answered. "It didn't quite last out. So they had to chance giving him straight N_2O. It worked. About as well as it does on us."

Justin whistled. "I guess everybody is asking how a creature from another world can be so similar to us?"

"And his uncle!"—this from Chester, sourly. "I've been drafted as your surrogate spokesman, and I'm not equipped. I think most of the people who've descended on us suspect me of being party to a high-powered confidence-trick."

That reminded Justin so acutely of what the other Chester had said, from the opposite point of view, that he felt the need to distract himself. He threw back the coverlet and swung his legs to the floor.

"The answer," he said, "is that he's not from another planet."

He had half-hoped that that might come as a bombshell. Instead, Cinnamon glanced at Chester and Herman, and they all nodded.

"We've come to pretty much the same conclusion," Cinnamon said. "But as for figuring out how it could happen—"

"Have you told everybody about your and my experience?" Justin interrupted.

She sighed. "In the end I had to. Most people have

taken it pretty well. Faced with the reality of the alien who isn't, they have damned little alternative. But there are some—General Lane, Admiral Clancy—who simply boiled over . . . I guess they must live in a finite universe."

That provoked chuckles all round.

"Well, as soon as you can get me next to a computer terminal," Justin said, "I think I may be able to tell you the answer to your question about how it could happen. You put me on the right track, Cinnamon, and now I'm over my shock—"

"Are you?" Herman murmured. "If half of what you and Cinnamon have said is true, won't it go on catching you by surprise for the rest of your lives?"

Justin had no immediate answer to that. Chester spoke up.

"I've had to cope with one complete and radical re-assessment of my life already. I told you about it. I swear, I'd never want to go by poster—not even if my house was burning down around my ears and a poster was the only escape! I could not face being cut adrift in a world where anything, without warning, could turn out to be different from what I used to know."

"You're on about that again?" Cinnamon demanded. "Justin, pay him no mind! I've been explaining to him that this is the way life is for just about everybody! It's a mysterious universal maze that we're picking our way through, and if you live on the primitive level you have one set of mysteries, and if you live on ours you have another, but basically it's—"

"Basically it's time for me to check over Dr. Williams and if he's okay send him for a shower and some breakfast," announced the young doctor firmly. "If he's to make your conference at oh-nine-hundred he'll need some solid food."

"Conference?" Justin said, glancing reflexively at a watch that wasn't there, then spotting it on the bedside shelf along with other personal items. It proved to be just on eight A.M.

"A complete review of everything that's known so far," Chester supplied. "It's going to be a daily event until they move the alien elsewhere. Right now he's too weak."

"I want to be there!" Justin declared. "And—doc! You're damned right. I'm starving hungry!"

"Fine. We'll see you there," Cinnamon said, turning to go. She checked. "But one more thing you ought to know in advance!"

He looked her a question.

"We have some more spinoff from the Gunther affair. Everyone who was there when he arrived, plus some post-mortem contacts, has contracted a completely new variety of influenza. So far it's not a killer. But they say that if it got to people who were already sickly or undernourished, it could well become a fatal epidemic."

Horrified, Justin said, "What about me? I was there too!"

"Cinnamon wouldn't let us forget it," Herman answered dryly. "But you're okay. We checked a blood-sample while you were out. You were there in the latent phase. None of them was infectious yet. It looks like droplet-transmission: coughing and sneezing."

"Or merely breathing," the young doctor capped. "Now are you going to move over or must I throw you out? Dr. Williams, what would you like from the canteen? Not, I guess, that I should be polite to you if you've wished a set of brand-new diseases on my already overtaxed profession."

That remark brought back to Justin with almost painful force the storm of disorganized thoughts which had been pouring through his head just before he collapsed. He was a little ashamed of giving way like that; he comforted himself with the reflection that nobody else he had ever heard of had had so much to endure—except the alien.

Correction: "alien." He compelled himself to put in mental quotation-marks. The creature shared a chromosome-count with humanity, not to mention its internal organs, its sexuality, its . . .

Its psychology? Only time would tell.

Mechanically relieving himself, showering, drying and dressing, he thought about one phrase which had been used: a computer transform of a human being. That would be about right. Suppose, for example, the operation of a poster were equivalent to a node in catastrophe theory. That was something he and Cinnamon ought to have evaluated, but because the reality—the *real* reality—of alternate universes was dismissed automatically from their minds, they had never bothered to invest computer-time in such speculation. But it must now be done. If the poster were ever to be constructively employed. But how could that be? With the limitation on the speed one could obtain information at, the destination must forever be unknowable. The poster could only grow into the biggest of all gambles, with the comforting overtone: it was impossible not to win as well as impossible not to lose.

By that stage his thinking was once more growing dreadfully confused. Grateful, he applied his attention to demolishing a pile of hotcakes with bacon and maple syrup. But even as he savored the food, he was struck by the inherent paradox of reality. What he was regarding, he felt justifiably, as the greatest event in history had lately taken place and an "alien" was somewhere right in this building. Here he was, likewise a visitor from another world, concerned with nothing more grandiose than breakfast. There ought to be a Chinese proverb on this subject. Maybe there was. If not, it deserved to be invented: how about this?

"Give a hungry man a pearl of great price, and he

will only ask whether there is food he may exchange it for."

Extended, that made far too much good sense for comfort. With Eustace and Inez and their colleagues, he had sensed excitement. He had dared to believe that this world was radically unlike his old one, where an event of that order was scheduled to occur shortly . . .

He almost dropped his fork.

Of course! An experiment in posting objects to and from orbit was due in his old world. If it were ever tried with a human being, inevitably something like what had happened here must result. The event would be witnessed by a Dr. Justin Williams.

Or would it? Would he have come from a more leisurely, more tolerant world like this one, and would he have found the new set-up unbearable, so that he was arrested as a security risk and interrogated and disbarred from further research—directly or indirectly, like the people from Project Ear?

Did universes spin off from every decision? If not, what rules governed their creation? Were there some where his counterpart, arriving from a kindlier world, was welcomed by a totalitarian system and encouraged to speak his mind? Were there universes he might have wound up in where rationality in the normal sense, even the law of logic, was unrecognizable? If the universe was indeed infinite, this must be so . . .

But here he grew dizzy. This was matter for philosophers, and would doubtless occupy them for centuries, unless this was a universe due to be disrupted by an unpredictable and illogical event which would destroy humanity. That kind of world must necessarily exist also. And so must every other. Every other!

Access from one to another, though, even given the poster or its equivalent—

Cursing, he realized he was once again following a mental path he had hoped to avoid. For the time being, the most urgent task before him was to keep his head and argue in reasoned terms with those who had not undergone the reality of being posted. The kind of transformation the process wrought was inevitably hard to credit. He must tread warily.

It was almost nine o'clock. He pushed away his empty breakfast-tray and made for the door.

FOURTEEN

the fossils of baked clay
inscribed with hebrew letters
the black pads of the toads
injected with india ink
enough of the true cross
to build another ark

For a long moment after entering Justin did not recognize this as the conference-room he and Cinnamon had been taken to on arrival. The table with its computer terminals had been replaced by rows of chairs, at least sixty of them, and three-quarters were already occupied. On a hastily-erected dais Inez and Eustace were rising to greet him; beside them were Herman, Levi, Chester and—thank goodness—Cinnamon.

In the front row, which was not so promising, sat General Lane, to whom Justin accorded a polite nod. But he smiled at Elaine Rotblat, who was three places distant.

Most of the people here, though, were total stangers.

He felt, once more, a giddying sensation. If it were the case that every decision spun off a new universe, then literally countless universes were being generated as people looked up to witness his entrance. More, with every step he took; more again, with every word he was to utter . . . He felt as though his mind were a house of cards in a high wind.

But it could not be that awful! He denied the possibility with all his willpower. Even if a decision taken by a stranger might undermine your dearest ambition, was that not the lot of humanity since the dawn of time? And it cut both ways: just as the conqueror marching over the hill might wreck the humble plans of a thousand villagers, so the dispassionate course of a disease might wipe him in his turn off the slate of history. That way went Alexander, surnamed Great.

The fact that he remembered being in a worse world, if not a very much worse one; the fact that Cinnamon had said the same, if on a smaller scale; the fact that obviously Gunther—the version who killed himself— must in both their original worlds have come from somewhere worse yet, all bolstered his shallow self-confidence as he confronted the audience.

Whether the alien had gone from a good to a bad world was yet to be established. But it was hard to imagine how being accidentally tossed among humans could be an improvement.

Maybe for every single one of the infinite possible total of universes there was a unique witness? Maybe solipsism was factual? But he balked at that. On the one hand, the universe he was best acquainted with included much too much he could not personally have become aware of (infinite regression loomed again at this point but he sternly dismissed it), while on the other this merely removed the problem from the aleph-two level to the aleph-one level. At least, he thought that was what it was doing; he would have to use a computer to be certain. He was no Georg Cantor.

At all events that was the least urgent aspect of the problem. Right now he had something far more difficult to do. He—with help from Cinnamon—must convey to the assembled experts on other subjects the basic principle of the poster, give a credible description of his and her experiences, and somehow make an explanation of the alien's appearance acceptable to them, when even he would have found it unbelievable a week ago.

Even with the help of a fulsome introduction from

Eustace Hamilton, who in this universe seemed to know a lot more about Justin's work than his counterpart in the other, it was not a prospect he relished.

Miraculously, however, at first it went very smoothly.

"Over the course of the past eight years, with the co-operation of Dr. Wright here and of other colleagues at Wright & Williams Inc., and with funding from the Chester Foundation, I have been developing a means of transferring material objects from one location to another effectively instantaneously. The device is conventionally termed a 'poster'. It is not"—he recalled Cinnamon's annoyance when Lane said people were being scrambled—"the matter transmitter familiar as a science-fiction prop. There is no direct communication between the dispatching and the receiving ends; the space within them is rendered congruent under the control of advanced computing systems and the location of the object being transferred becomes indefinite, so that it so to say shuttles from one to the other. By cancelling the congruity when the object is in the receptor, it is made to appear to undertake a physical journey. The process requires considerable expenditure of power, but it is very efficient and the amount of degraded energy, such as heat, which ensues is almost literally negligible.

"At this point I should familiarize you with the term 'rho-space', a convenient fiction we have adopted much as, say, the concept of the neutrino was adopted when there was no means of detecting it if it existed. It happens to be essential to reconcile certain anomalies in the observed phenomena—for instance, that the transferred object, although arriving so far as we can tell at the speed of light, does not acquire infinite mass in so doing. Forgive my use of 'instantaneously' just now, by the way. I'm sure you'll have realized that what I meant was: instantaneously as nearly as the speed-of-light limitation permits us to establish.

"By invoking a hypothetical space which contacts our

own at every point but at right angles—a fairly conventional image, I think you'll agree—we found it possible to obtain solutions for the basic equations we had developed, which were interpretable in the form of hardware. Much to our amazement, I may say. Right up to the moment we carried out our first successful test, transferring a few grams of matter across the width of this room, we were still half-convinced that while the logic of our computations was unassailable some bug in the real world would prevent it working."

A few people chuckled at that point. Justin began to relax.

"This being a novel and very expensive technique, support had to be found from sources in addition to the Chester Foundation. I won't go into details"—just as well, Justin reflected wryly, because those details might not match—"but I can say it was successfully used for transferring sensitive intelligence data to and from embassies abroad. The first hint that anything might be amiss came when an agent, the first to be transferred over such a distance—though volunteers, naturally, had undergone the experience previously—this agent, as I say, arrived in a deranged condition and . . . Well, committed suicide on arrival.

"This appalled us, since not only the volunteers I just mentioned but also Dr. Wright had been posted without apparent ill-effects. I myself insisted on being posted over the same distance as the agent, though in the opposite direction, and as a direct result stumbled on the key to what is really happening when a poster transfer occurs. It would be hard for me to make you believe that I arrived in a world radically different from the one I left, but for one stroke of fortune which I shall come to in a moment. I don't yet know how completely altered this world is, compared with what I remember, but I can say, for instance, that back there T. Emory Chester is a grasping, self-seeking politician instead of a world-renowned philanthropist; funding for the poster project came not wholly from the Chester Foundation but predominantly from the Defense Department; and this country is suffering its worst recession since the 1930's."

Signs of incredulity and bafflement were to be seen on at least half the faces now, and on a few, including Lane's, outright hostility. But he carried doggedly on.

"Dr. Wright, so it turns out, has experienced something similar though far less acute, while I am certain the same will be found to hold true of the earlier volunteers. Professor Tesch, I haven't asked, but I assume you've taken steps to trace them all?"

Levi, half-rising, nodded emphatically. And added, "If I may interrupt for a moment, Justin? Thanks. I only want to say that it's been suggested I put you and Cinnamon—Dr. Wright—under hypnosis to establish how complete your impressions are of the other worlds you remember."

"You mean someone is still prepared to think of it as hallucination?" Justin said in genuine astonishment. "With the so-called alien right here on the base with us?"

"So-called?" somebody said from the back of the hall in a stage-whisper, precisely pitched for maximum audibility. Justin snatched at it.

"Yes, so-called! Dr. Rotblat!" He turned to Elaine. "Before I flaked out from fatigue, I'd been told that this creature, apart from being an oxygen-breather, has a chromosome count of 46 like ours. Subsequently it's been operated on by a human surgeon, withstood an anaesthetic used on human beings—"

"You can add the fact," Elaine said clearly, "that he took a massive transfusion of human plasma. We couldn't give whole blood—he turns out to be a non-O recipient—but his plasma is identical with ours down to the molecular level."

Thinking, prematurely, that his point had been made,

Justin turned back to his listeners with a flourish. But from all over the hall there were cries and waves.

"What's all this about an alien? We only just got here! Are you all crazy? Tripping on something? Nobody told us about aliens!"

The meeting was about to get completely out of hand. Eustace started to rise, a call to order on his lips, but Inez checked him with a touch on his arm and stood up herself.

"Order! *Order!* We up here want to know what they did tell you that persuaded you to come along!"

There was a blank pause. One of the newcomers said eventually, "Well, that there was an emergency and I was needed."

"Same here," came a cry, and another, the near-echo of it.

"So you weren't told that in the first-ever attempt to post a human being back from orbit Ed Landini went in up there and something different with the same injuries as he had came out down here?"

Lane was on his feet, shouting, but his words were lost in the general clamor until he marched forward and seized a microphone from in front of Chester.

"Silence!" he roared. Gradually the hubbub quieted. He went on, "I must impress on you that what you have just been told must not be mentioned to anybody outside this room! The existence of the poster project is classified, let alone its space applications—"

Chester rose, leaned across the table, and neatly plucked the microphone out of Lane's hand. He said musingly to it, "And people like that expect you to help them with this kind of problem?" He stressed the pronouns just enough.

A loud, slightly forced laugh; it came from Inez. It was taken up. In seconds the atmosphere was altered. In a good humor again, people resumed their places. His face thunderous, Lane spun on his heel and strode out.

"There goes trouble," Chester murmured. "But the floor is yours again, Justin. How do you account for what's happened?"

"Ah . . ." Wiping his brow, Justin picked up the thread. "I suspect that rho-space must have objective reality. I accept that the congruence of the space within two posters cannot be precise. It extends to an infinite number of other spaces: as nearly as I can guess, to aleph-three such spaces, and conceivably this may be what aleph-four counts. Anyone unfamiliar with Cantorian transfinites had better get a briefing on them. In the case of inanimate objects this doesn't seem to matter. It probably matters very little in the case of lower animals. But when it comes to a live human being it's very significant. Consciousness seems to be a fundamental factor.

"We postulate that there is a direct relationship between the distance in our space over which a human being is posted, and the divergence of what you get back from your original. The greater the distance, the more skewed the version which arrives. We have a red-blooded oxygen-breathing biped wearing a spacesuit as evidence. It's rather as though the computers operating the poster become more and more eager to grasp at a resemblance. Maybe this relates to the standard uncertainty principle. As yet I didn't find time to investigate."

"But it fits," Cinnamon muttered behind him. "It fits too damned well for comfort!"

Now the audience was once more showing disbelief. Whispered conversations were breaking out all over the room. After a moment a tall man near the back rose to his feet. Seeming to voice what everyone was thinking, he said, "You're talking about the existence of multiple realities, right?"

"I guess so," Justin admitted.

"Then I for one want to see this alien, so-called or not!"

There was a rattle of applause. Someone else said, "And if it's true that posting changes people out of recognition, you'd better stop posting them. Right now, and for good!"

"Who's that?" Justin muttered to Chester, and was answered with a shrug expressive of ignorance.

"But you'd better quiet him before there's a ban-the-poster movement!"

Marshalling his words, Justin was prevented from speaking again, however. Elaine wore a doctor's call-phone around her neck. It beeped loudly, and she set it to her ear. After a few seconds she said to it, "I'll be right there!"

And, rising, she addressed the room at large.

"Lord only knows what this means, but I just got a call from the infirmary.

"Our red-blooded biped wearing a spacesuit, as Justin accurately describes him, woke up a couple of minutes ago. And spoke to the nurses on duty.

"In plain English."

There was a dead silence. Since no one else seemed ready to put the crucial question, Justin finally spoke up.

"What did he say?"

Elaine licked her lips. "Something like: 'I never saw people like you before. I guess this must be your first time, right?' "

FIFTEEN

the image of cho/ice
either trudge another hour
through the bitterest night of winter
to reach the usual bridge
or take a short cut homeward
and in mid-river hear crack . . . crack . . .

All the security demanded by Lane and Clancy—all the precautions imposed by the medical staff—*nothing* could have stopped the assembled scientists from mobbing their way into the infirmary. Herman shouted warnings about contagion, Levi tried to block the exit from the conference-room, and the tide of bodies swept them aside. Justin and Cinnamon exchanged despairing glances. There was nothing for it but to tag along with the rest.

Justin at least was relieved. By this stage in his address he had begun to feel the need for concrete evidence, seen with his own eyes and heard with his own ears, to bolster the increasingly flimsy-seeming argument he had advanced.

And the outbreak of a new kind of 'flu could have been coincidental . . .

Once they were in the familiar authoritarian surroundings of the hospital, though, the frenzy subsided. Alarmed doctors, surgeons and nurses who emerged into the main hallway as though expecting to confront a lynch-mob, met only with a defiant demand to be allowed to see the alien.

"Oh, sure you can see him!" the senior doctor exclaimed. "Two at a time and for a minute only, through glass! We have to keep him in sterile conditions until we've cultivated the organisms he brought with him. But . . ."

He hesitated, his eyes scanning the crowd.

"But just before I came out he said that if this is a typical scenario, the inventors of the poster should be here. If so, he wants to talk to them. Are they?"

Typical scenario?

There was something obscurely terrifying about that phrase. Justin caught Cinnamon's hand and thrust his way forward, as much to quiet the disturbance it had conjured up in his mind as because he was eager to see the alien in the flesh.

Or talk to him.

Before they had pushed to the front, Lane and Clancy had completed a whispered discussion. The former spoke up loudly.

"It must be a hoax! It can't be anything else!"

All eyes turned on him.

"The idea of this being an alien creature when it speaks English!" Lane amplified, while Clancy vigorously nodded her agreement.

"But I assure you, General—" began the senior doctor.

"It's nonsensical! I don't know what the hell the game is, but I'm not going to be taken in! I'm going straight to the President. I want authority to put this place under full-scale martial law so we can find out what sort of damn-fool trickery is going on."

"Did I hear that right?" came a question from the far end of the hallway. Chester forced a way forward, eyes very wide and somewhat red for lack of sleep.

"Yes, *sir!*"

Arriving in front of Lane, Chester looked him up and down for a few seconds, then shrugged.

"Try if you like. I don't imagine you'll get any higher

than I got. The President is on vacation in Honolulu, you know."

Clearly Lane had forgotten. His face fell.

"But I reached the Secretary of State," Chester continued. "He's less sceptical. He appointed me *pro-tem.* envoy and spokesman to deal with our alien friend. By tonight he hopes to replace me with a career diplomat, a philosopher and one of the people who authorized Project Ear. Well?"

Under his breath the general muttered something which might have been, "Damn' civilians!"

Chester ignored his reaction. Smiling rather shyly, he made his way closer to Cinnamon and Justin, both of whom clapped him on the shoulder.

"While I enjoy my unexpected office," he said loudly and clearly, "I want to benefit from it. Doctor, is it safe for the alien to be interviewed?"

"Well, I guess if you're gowned and masked . . ."

It was obvious that the alien found difficulty in breathing; his chest was strapped to protect his broken ribs, but now and then he winced and those curious eyes screwed up in perfectly human fashion.

Surveying the uniformly-clad visitors who had now entered the ward, he said, "Which of you are the inventors and which is the official spokesman?"

His voice was peculiar; it had a kind of harsh, barking quality—due to his injuries or not, it was impossible to guess. But apart from that his speech was entirely comprehensible.

How could that be so? *How?*

Rising superbly to the occasion, Chester solemnly introduced himself and his companions, and concluded by asking: "And what may be your name—sir?"

"Why . . ." The alien blinked. "Ed Landini, of course. Or Dr. Eduardo Landini if you want to be more formal. What did you expect me to be called?"

There was a moment of blank silence. The doctor and

nurse who were also in the ward exchanged looks of near-horror.

Then the alien sighed in a completely human fashion.

"Oh dear. Oh *dear!* I never expected to get quite so far away from my main line on such a short transfer. I really did expect to wind up among something more like my own people. Not that it matters, of course, whatever becomes of me."

Justin, clenching fingers into palms, took half a pace nearer. He hazarded a wild guess at the creature's meaning.

"Is that—could that be—because you've learned to accept that there are, objectively, many versions of you?"

"Well, naturally. I've known since I was old enough to read that I exist in at least aleph-null versions, and there may very well be more than that who have something in common with me. You haven't reached that stage of awareness yet?"

His listeners shook their heads as one.

"I *am* in trouble, then . . . Let's make the best of it." He winced as he reflexively tried to adjust his position, only to find himself constrained by the harness securing his injured pelvis. "If you haven't given me anything to prevent itching," he added, "please do! I'm chemically matched to you to about twenty decimal places. Must be, or your poster would never have collected me, right? You do have anti-prurients, I suppose? Sometimes the oddest things get overlooked in medicine, they say."

Nervous, the nurse brought an appropriate lotion, and let it trickle down inside the harness. Watching, Justin felt an electrical tingle all over his own skin. So far, everything he had heard the alien say—no, correction: make that Dr. Landini!—was amazingly close to what he would have expected had his friend from his former world been lying in this bed. Hints and tantalizing clues sparkled on the surface of his mind like darting fireflies, but refused to settle and make a pattern he could analyze.

They would. They would eventually. For the time being he was content to let the alien guide him. It was plain that he understood far more of what was happening than anybody else present. Come to that, than anybody else in this version of Earth.

"What about offering my visitors some chairs?" Landini resumed. "All this is being recorded, I take it? Yes? And I likewise assume someone has remembered to organize a computer remote, because your medical standards are five or ten years behind the ones I'm used to and if the rest of your science is commensurate—which doesn't follow—then you're going to need all sorts of props and metaphors and analogies."

The moment a chair was provided for her, Cinnamon swept it up one-handed, swung it around, and set it close alongside the bed. She took the alien's hand in both of hers and leaned earnestly towards him.

"Even if there are aleph-null of you, you don't have to strain to keep up the act, you know. Our version of Ed Landini must be going through something far worse, if he's wound up in your universe, but even so—"

The harsh voice interrupted. "You're kind, and I'm grateful. Though you must surely realize that the chances of him winding up where I came from are reciprocal aleph-one. *Is* that computer on the way? We surely need it. I'm only a lowly rigger, pretty much the same type of person who used to work in the oilfields or the South American railroads. I don't have half the information I know you're going to want. Still, I promise I'll do my best. Just let me start out by checking what scenario this is."

"I thought you knew," Chester exclaimed. "You asked which of us were the inventors, which the spokesman—"

"Oh, man!" the creature sighed. (Once more Justin forced himself to think again, making it: Landini sighed.) "I guess I never understood in my guts before what a difference the invention of posters makes to your world-view. Look, friend, the *class* of scenario is easy enough to identify. You're first-timers and you speak English, and I'm here, and all that adds up to a schema pretty much like what happened in my world-cluster a generation ago. The discovery of the posting effect is pretty skew, you know . . . What am I saying? You don't know, or I wouldn't have to spell it out for you like this."

He licked his lips with a tongue that seemed quite human although rather long and narrow. By now Justin was finding it hard to remember that this was physically a non-human face; the voice was so persuasive.

"But beyond that—well, I've heard about fifty or a hundred different developments stemming from this sort of set-up, and of course I know in my head there are an infinity of infinities of them . . . Look, you start. You ask me the most burning questions and that'll limit things considerably."

Prompt, Chester said, "How is it, since you're physically different from us, that you speak English and answer to a name we're—ah—familiar with?"

"Oh, man," Landini said in a lugubrious tone, "you really didn't get near the point yet, did you? I'm here *because* I speak English, *because* I'm called Landini, *because* I was working on a satellite and got crushed by a girder and the only chance of saving my life was to post me back to the surface."

"You mean it was a choice between dying and being kicked out of your own universe?" Cinnamon suggested.

"Lady, you are coming a lot closer now. A lot closer. I never got posted before, because I don't have the temperament for it—I mean, I'm not a pilgrim or a mystic, just a good average handyman with an engineering degree to make me sound fancier than I am—but what with the pain and the blood I was coughing up

and the mess I could feel in my belly . . . You hit it:
I'd have taken any chance in the universe to go on
living. I remember as they packed me into the poster
I was wondering what my old lady would be like when
I met her again. I sure hope"—this with a mirthless
chuckle—"my namesake here is a bachelor, because
I'd be kind of a shock to someone your shape, hm?"

"He's orphaned and unmarried!" Justin exclaimed
promptly, thinking of the Landini he had known who
worked on Project Ear. As soon as the word escaped
he was transfixed by fear of being contradicted, because
that Landini did not belong to *this* universe.

And was contradicted—immediately, but not disas-
trously. Chester said, frowning, "There was some reference in the news yesterday to a woman friend, but
I don't know whether he filed a next-of-kin status for
her . . . Still, I guess she can be told he's dead if all
else fails."

"Figures!" the alien sighed. "The usual kind of lies
and distortions I was told people in my position had to
put up with."

"But I don't see how you can speak English when
you're . . . !" The doctor had stepped forward, intending to make what to him was plainly the most important
point of all, but now he broke off as though afraid what
he had it in mind to say might sound offensive.

"When I'm obviously descended from a different
branch of the primates?" Landini supplied, and on receiving a nod did his best to shrug. "Far as I'm concerned, that's standard too. Do you have creatures that
look as though they could have been my ancestors?"

From a dry mouth Justin said, "We probably call
them baboons."

"Mm-hm. That's what we call the creatures who look
more like you than they look like me. They can't exist
here because you do."

"But how *can* you speak English?" the doctor insisted.

"And how can I hail from a world where there are countries called America and Russia and China and Egypt? Because in fact that's so . . . Do you know, Dr. Williams?"

Justin shook his head. His throat was too tight to speak through.

"Well, it's because they exist, and even if you can't perceive them, your machines by this time *can*."

SIXTEEN

between ranges of hills
a straight fast road
welcome to car and driver
at the last moment
meeting no resistance
brake   down

By now reluctantly convinced that they really could treat the readings the monitors gave for their improbable patient as though he were an ordinary human person, the medical staff put a stop to the discussion at that point on the valid grounds that Landini was too weak to continue. As well as coping with the interrogation, he had had to put up with a constant stream of curious faces peering at him through an observation window at the far side of the ward, like a specimen in a zoo.

No matter how calm and collected he might sound, the predicament he had wound up in must be intolerable. Cinnamon recognized the fact, and murmured to one of the nurses as she and Justin reached the door, "Make sure he's given something against shock, won't you? I saw what it did to my friend here, and . . . and his case is far, far worse."

Justin squeezed her hand affectionately and she gave him a sad smile.

As though the alien's arrival had been a missile puncturing a soap-bubble which burst with majestic deliberateness, the next week turned into a sequence of repetitions on an ever-larger scale climaxing in a wet droplet of diffusing scepticism.

Such images were much on Justin's mind during it. Catastrophe theory—four- and five- and even six-dimensional equivalents of the conventional universe, curved so as to be boundless but not infinite—above all Cantorian transfinites, the numbers capable of counting more events or objects than there was room for in the known universe, which by this time seemed on the verge of being converted into a useful tool, just as Clerk Maxwell's equations had been when electricity ceased to be a laboratory marvel and turned into a commonplace.

Trapped here in Texas, yet half afraid of being sent away, he and Cinnamon wrestled, in company with their friends, against the angel of incredulity. Miraculously, despite the fact that it was impossible to hide the absence of so many distinguished people from their ordinary posts, the truth of what was happening was kept from the media and hence from other national governments; however, each day saw a new horde of experts descending on this isolated outpost, and each group in turn demanded time with Landini and the chance to convince themselves this was not what—against all odds—General Lane and Admiral Clancy were still maintaining: a hoax . . . But less and less attention was paid to them as time went by.

Although they were no longer permitted to see Landini except when he positively insisted on sending for them—and that happened only twice during the week—Justin and Cinnamon kept in touch with the snippets of information which were added to what they already possessed, thanks to the daily meetings which reviewed a computer-abridged summary of what Landini had said and then degenerated into dozens of private arguments. The worst problem came from a handful of Christians who had been invited to join the team; they proved to be fundamentalist to a man, and Landini in their terms was necessarily a tool of Satan. The fact that he admitted to being a non-practicing Catholic aggravated matters . . .

Here, though, was the eye of the storm. Repercussions were radiating on the national and international scale, and all poster operations were currently forbidden, and the foreign eavesdroppers who were always listening to signals from the Polly were piecing fact after unbelievable fact together and very soon were bound to reach an inevitable conclusion, but there was still time to debate and reason, and Cinnamon and Justin and Chester and Herman and Levi and, thanks to their prior acquaintance, Inez and Eustace, took every chance they got to sit down quietly with a well-connected computer remote and batter their brains against the wall of inconsistencies implicit in everything that Landini the alien had said . . . indeed, in everything he *was*.

Of the three people the President assigned as his representatives, the diplomat most disturbed Justin. He was the ambassador who had bestowed such a lavish compliment just before his poster trip. But in this world his career had taken a different course, and they had never met.

The member of the committee that authorized Project Ear proved to be Geary Fowler, whom they had already met—and who, behind his austere façade, concealed a genuine sense of excitement about the possibility of contacting alien intelligence. But he wanted it to be *alien*. Once satisfied that this one spoke English as a mother-tongue, and that it was not a hoax, he lost interest; one day he simply faded from the scene and never reappeared.

Since the diplomat seemed incapable of making the mental leap involved in accepting aliens, and was more concerned about using posters for intelligence work, that left the third of the newcomers in a position of considerable authority. Luckily she turned out to be a catalyst.

Edna Bloughram, professor of philosophy, was known to all of them by name; she was a woman of about sixty with an unworldly manner, grey hair and heavy glasses, whom Levi had met at more than one conference on the relation between perception and reality, and who had published a couple of books with sufficient news-value to turn her into a TV pundit, summoned when An Authority was indicated.

She proved to be one of those people who mask a basic shyness with an acerb directness, but betray the strain it costs in a quavering voice. Having been through the initial routine of questioning Landini, and reviewed the record of his sayings prior to her arrival, she gratefully seized on Levi's offer—their prior meetings endowing him with the status of "old friend"—to sneak away and meet the inventors of the poster. Having a slight edge over late-comers, Justin and Cinnamon had by now created a cosy almost-home for themselves in the barrack-block which had been pressed into service for the exploding population. Many were worse off; there were sand-filled tents that froze at night . . .

And they began to talk sense together straight away.

"So you've learned this much from the alien! Why not more?"

"Because he's only an engineer, not a speculative philosopher," Cinnamon replied.

"Then why haven't you drafted some outline hypotheses to see if he recognizes them and can fill in the rest of the details?"

"Apart from anything else," Justin sighed, "those details may not match our universe."

Edna snorted. "That can't be right! Surely the whole essence of his being selected lies in the world-view his brain held at the time of transfer?"

There was a dead silence in the small and crowded room which Justin and Cinnamon were sharing, broken only by the noise of yet another plane landing, and the chink of ice on glass as Herman mixed himself a *Cuba libre*. Even that stopped when the words sank in.

"Can I please hear that again slowly?" Justin requested.

"I'd have thought it was obvious." Edna hunched forward, raising long bony fingers to count off the points she was making—or maybe scoring. "You've told me there is necessarily an infinitely good chance that any poster we put into operation in our usual world is a better match for one in another world than it is for the intended one. In passing, I can't help saying I wish I'd been consulted when you were designing the damned thing!"

"We didn't design it," Justin said after a momentary hesitation. Cinnamon tensed, on the point of raising an objection; suddenly she saw his point, and gave a glum nod.

"What? Oh! You mean because it's a four-color problem?"

"Much worse," Justin said. "Much, *much* worse. But the human brain certainly can't cope. It calls for computers. Our—our *new friend* Landini takes this for granted, he says."

"Even so, some of the implications— Never mind. What matters is that when only an inanimate object is in the field of the poster, the transfer takes place and nobody notices a discrepancy. Right?"

They all nodded.

"When an animate person is in the field, the discrepancy is glaring right away, correct?"

"Not quite right away, but . . ." Cinnamon bit her lip. "Yes, I have to grant that."

"And we've traced our original four volunteers now," Levi chimed in. "We have two broken marriages and two addicts to explain away, when we carefully selected them in the first place for maximal social stability. I'm betting on the sense of vague disorientation which resulted from shifting to a different world." He shuddered. "I'm alarmed to find you taking it so calmly, Edna."

"I haven't been posted," was her tart response. "And I haven't lived in a stable universe since I was a child! Where were we . . . ? Oh, yes. A transfer on the surface of this planet where there are necessarily a lot of humans in a particular zone of nearby space results in a minor discrepancy. The first from orbit gives us *not* a disturbed human but an alien speaking English with a human metabolism and a human name."

Throwing her hands in the air, she looked—or rather glared—at her listeners.

"Well, what does that spell out to you?"

"Half a dozen things," Justin said at once. "I'm afraid I don't see any way to choose between them."

"Such as—?"

"Well, that there's a skewed but consistent relationship between distance covered and the type of—uh—person delivered."

"But type in what sense?"

"On the present evidence, English-speaking and forty-six-chromosomal and—"

"But how can an alien speak English?" Herman burst out.

"He's not an alien!" Edna snapped. "Justin knows that, don't you?"

With a miserable nod: "That was the first truth I cottoned on to. And . . ." He tensed, excitedly. "And now I think I see what *you* mean by calling him 'not an alien'. Lord! How many dimensions do we have to think in, though, to make sense of this lot?"

"About seven," was Edna's composed opinion. "Think on this level first: there are creatures speaking English whose world history matches ours one-for-one despite"—a scowl at Herman who was visibly framing an objection—"the unlikelihood of creatures with different palatal formations, faces, cranial structure, skeletal proportions, having a Julius Caesar and an Attila the Hun in their past."

"You established—?" Cinnamon began.

"No, of course I didn't," Edna said crossly. "I simply don't find any difficulty in taking it for granted that this version of Landini must have that in his history, because—"

"Because otherwise English could never arise as a language," Levi proposed.

"No! Because otherwise he could never have turned up in one of our posters!"

There was another thoughtful pause.

"I'd been thinking about that," Cinnamon said, reaching for the keyboard of the computer remote and tapping in the interrogation code for the main poster program. It was no longer so easy to reach it as it had been before the alien appeared. Owing to the enormous investment of both public funds and Chester Foundation money in the project, restrictions had been imposed. But from here it was still fairly accessible.

Chester, who had been brooding in what had become his usual corner, stirred and spoke up.

"I'm impressed by the way you're accepting what you've been told," he said to Edna. "But you seem to be making—what to call it?—a poster-jump of your own! As near as I can figure, you're requiring that the creature in the poster, the one that turns up instead of what's expected, must be the one who regards the universe as nearly the same as the—well, the original."

"That's right," Edna declared emphatically.

"I don't know much about your work, but the few

things I've read, and what I've heard you say on television, make me believe that you're basically a subjec-
tivist, a sort of post-Berkeleian."

"Fair enough," Edna agreed, while Cinnamon whispered a quick summary of the views of Bishop Berke-
ley for the benefit of a puzzled Herman.

"So it follows," Chester pursued, "that the universe
is real insofar as it is perceived?"

"I'd have to concur."

"But Landini—I mean, *our* Landini—couldn't very
well have had any conception of a poster permitting
him to be dumped in another world. So why did he
not arrive back in our regular universe?"

He sat back with a smug expression. It rapidly
vanished.

"He probably did!" Edna exploded. "We're counting
in terms of Cantorian transfinites, with absolutely no
way of detecting which out of infinitely many human
Landinis wound up in recognizable worlds, and how
many inhuman ones did the same."

"You're saying Ed Landini—"

"*Did* get home," Justin broke in. "He must have
done! An infinite number of times over! With all possible shades of difference in between!"

"But this doesn't hold water," Levi said. "If the correspondence between the posters depends, as Edna
claims, on the perceived nature of reality—in other
words, if you make the posters' internal spaces congruent to the nth degree, what dictates the choice of
arrival-point is the world-view held in the subject's
brain—if *that* is so, how can any alien like the one
we've received ever turn up in a foreign universe? The
compatibility . . ."

His voice tailed away. Edna, smiling, gave a nod.

"I think we just saw someone get the point. You got
it already, Justin, didn't you?"

Out of a dry mouth he said, "It must depend not on our perception but on what the computers perceive."

"Of course it must. And I bet when we ask alien-Landini whether this is so, he'll tell us yes, of course."

Which, with an air of genuine astonishment, he did.

SEVENTEEN

> groggily awakening
> in France or Italy or Spain
> turning the tap marked C
> intending a cold-water wash
> forgetting that the other one says F
> and being scalded

"How does it feel to be an entry in some machine's data-bank?"

The question startled Justin and Cinnamon as they wheeled a cart down the aisles of the supermarket created yesterday to serve what had naturally been baptized "Instant City". There was no place on earth where the population was exploding so rapidly; the past week had seen the arrival of nearly six thousand people, and because matters were arranged slightly differently here than in Justin's former world there had apparently to be room for private enterprise. Hence this prefabricated six-aisle market with its produce still chilled not from deliberate freezing but from high-altitude flight.

It was crowded. To all its customers, as well as to Justin and Cinnamon for particular reasons, it came as a welcome breath of normality.

To be cherished. There might be little of it left.

"Why—why, Herman!" Cinnamon exclaimed, in the slightly shrill tone she had been using more and more during the past few days. Her eyes were too large and too round, also, and her palms were always sweaty and sometimes her hand shook enough to spill the contents of a cup or glass. Justin had not mentioned the fact to her, although he had never lived with anyone before, not even his wife in the other world, in such proximity. They were still lodged in the same narrow room, still forbidden to leave Texas and return to Chester U, still more crowded by the day as Cinnamon specified additional equipment for their home terminals. There were three now, each compact by its designer's standards, but each spawning sub-assemblies that not even microminiaturization could prevent from piling up in head-high stacks.

They were looking for an alternative to the idea which had just been expressed, and failing completely.

"Where've you been?" Justin said roughly.

Herman sighed. He had dark rings of tiredness under his dark eyes. "If you'd been interested enough to want to know, you wouldn't be asking now," he said after a fraught pause.

Hot rage boiled up at the back of Justin's throat. He felt his hands tighten absurdly on the handles of the cart. Cinnamon, distracted, was searching nearby shelves for some gourmet item which the supermarket stock-computer would no doubt have accorded minimum priority.

"Don't you have any idea what it's like here now?" he demanded in a barely-controlled whisper. "You must have been to hell and back, and I mean *back!*"

A trifle alarmed by the intensity of the reaction he had provoked, Herman flinched and smiled insincerely.

"You really didn't know they seconded Elaine and me to clear up the outbreak of alien 'flu?"

"Oh, was that it?" Cinnamon spun around, still empty-handed. "Is there going to be an epidemic? And why you?"

"Me? Oh, because I'd been told about posters, what else? And that did me no good at all in the upshot, because it went under to standard vaccines and no, there won't be an epidemic."

His eyes flicking from one to other of their faces, Herman hesitated.

"You make it sound as though things have gone badly here while I was away. But I was told—"

"Oh, sure, I bet you were!" Cinnamon said in a brittle tone. "And it's true. Landini is a perfect patient for the infirmary staff. He even tried making a dirty joke to one of the nurses yesterday. Instead of being ashamed and shutting up, she shared it with the girl who was next on duty, and by now it's clear across the site! By tomorrow I bet one of them will have tried screwing him!"

By chance, that peaking cry emerged into a lull. On all sides people selecting goods or waiting for checkout turned their heads; some registered pleased surprise on recognizing Justin, or Cinnamon, or Herman, or all three.

"Screwing someone with a pelvic fracture," Herman said after a pause, "is not approved medical practice."

"He doesn't have a pelvic fracture any more," Justin said sourly.

"What?"

"It's the truth, I'm afraid. Weren't you there when he said our medical techniques were five or ten years out of date? Seems he was right. They have a trick with ultra-low frequency radiation which heals bone so fast you can almost see it happening."

"ULF bone therapy is no news to us!" Herman parried indignantly.

"Maybe not," Justin muttered. "But to him it's so much a matter of routine, he was able to compile from memory the kind of program you need to run the treatment—and he's not even a doctor, he's a structural engineer!"

"For him, apparently," Cinnamon supplemented, "it's a habit like—oh—memorizing your blood-group, or your allergies."

"So he's up and about, is he?" Herman said after taking a moment to digest the news.

"Sure. We've invited him to a party this evening."

"What?"

"Why not? He's bored in that hospital ward, same as you or I would be, now his ribs and pelvis have mended. And he isn't a philosopher, so he's bored with what Edna has been saying, and he's not a poster technician, so he's had all he can take of what Justin and I have been asking . . ." She shrugged. "Stuck in this foreign universe, he's not going to have much fun for the rest of his life, but at least we can give him the chance to relax and chat about something else."

By now there was a crowd of forty or fifty people gathered within earshot. A young man with fair hair strode forward.

"You're having a party for the alien? But General Lane and Admiral Clancy both told us he had to be kept isolated because of the risk of infection—"

"Lane? Clancy?" Cinnamon put her hand to her mouth as to stifle a giggle. "Know what they're about right now? Go on, Massa Justin! Tell 'em de *troof!*"

Under the surprised gaze of the onlookers, Justin said, "Trying to save the Earth from an invasion from a parallel world."

"Justin, that's not funny—" began Herman.

"I'm glad you agree!" Justin flared. "What risk of infection is there? Did you check when you got back from stamping out this 'flu epidemic that wasn't?"

Taken aback, Herman said, "Why—why, yes! They say none of the organisms he brought with him is resistant to our antibiotics. At any rate, not in culture."

"So he's coming to our party tonight," Cinnamon said in triumph, leaning on Justin's shoulder as she dumped the latest of her purchases in the already laden cart.

"Where is it? When?" demanded the young man with fair hair. A score of others pressed forward, putting

the same question. Justin raised himself on tiptoe, one
hand supporting him on Cinnamon's shoulder.

"I'd like to invite you all!" he shouted. "But I'm not
allowed to—although, I guess, if we did invite everyone
we'd have to keep the party running for a month and
still you wouldn't all have had a chance to say hello . . .
And I'm only the *invento*r of the fucking poster, right?"

His declamation climaxed on a near-sob, and Cinnamon caught his hand.

"It's all right," he said in a dull voice when he had
recovered. "But I don't want to go the way of all the
others."

"What does he mean?" Herman hissed at Cinnamon.

"According to Landini, in an infinite cluster of the
universes where this happens, the inventors of the poster
go insane," she returned in an equally soft voice.

"What?"

"Goddammit, man, haven't you realized yet that this
son-of-an-alien bitch comes from a world where this
sort of thing is commonplace?"

"What sort of thing? Why haven't we heard about
it?"—this, from the fair-haired young man and a half-
dozen others thrusting forward with him. "You mean
the arrival of aliens?"

"The invitation of aliens!" Justin shouted. "The
space-lab he was working on wasn't like ours! It was
to launch more and more posters outwards into interstellar space, so that whenever any of them was activated, someone from a different continuum would turn
up!"

"But," Herman began in dismay, "surely you must
have an equivalent in the dispatching poster, and if
that holds good—"

"They're ahead of us!" Justin blasted. "There's no
lack of volunteers! They call them pilgrims! That's why
our Dr. Landini is so sane—he says he was never
tempted to be a pilgrim, but he can't help admiring

that sort of person, so now it's happened to him accidentally, he can't feel too bad about it."

"He would have liked to be—to be swapped for a stranger?" Herman forced out.

"Oh, not really! But he's resigned to it, because there are so many of him!"

"So many," Cinnamon echoed greyly. She looked along the ranks of interchangeable cans and packages on the market's shelves. "More than those, infinitely more . . . But not in our perception-range. More as though we were stock in the electronic register of this company's computers."

The fair-haired young man said, after a brief hesitation, "If there's going to be a party for the alien, we'd like—"

"I'm sure you would," barked Justin. "But I dare not invite you. Weren't you *listening?* Cinnamon and I are dead lucky we can hold this party—not that I'm looking forward to it much any more. It's going to be recorded and analyzed and spied on . . . But Landini says that's the way it usually goes, and we have to believe him."

"Usually?"—from someone at the back of the crowd.

"Yes, usually!" Cinnamon flared. "He grew up with this! He knows what happens when a first-timer leaks into another universe! His world has had a dozen of them!"

"Darling, if you go on like this," Justin muttered, taking her hand, "you know we'll be arrested, don't you?"

"I guess so," she sighed, turning away. "Make like fuzz and clear this bunch . . . Herman!" Suddenly she clutched his arm and spoke in a fierce whisper.

"Invasion from a parallel world?" someone said as the crowd dispersed. "Are they all insane?"

"Be at the party tonight!" Cinnamon begged. "I shall need someone's shoulder to cry on, or—I swear—both me and Justin, we'll live out the prediction the son-of-a-bitch has made, and by dawn we'll both be certifiably insane!"

"What prediction?" Herman countered, baffled.

"That we're doomed, of course! He's been right on every other point so far, and he says our going mad is *normal*."

EIGHTEEN

on the label it said
safe when used as directed
why then this giddiness
numbness and nausea
with sick realization
you must be allergic

"In a way," said Chester thoughtfully to Justin, "I guess this is the proper way to celebrate the end of the world."

The party, held in the only sizable room available—the conference-room—had been his idea, and his money underwrote the catering. The suggestion had been approved, cautiously, by the experts in charge; it seemed like an excellent idea to try out alien-Landini in a normal social situation before he was—inevitably—exposed to the world. This big a secret could not be kept forever.

But, partly at least thanks to Cinnamon and Justin's encounter with Herman in the supermarket, the original plan, to assemble not more than a dozen people for a meal and a few beers, had had to be drastically revised. There were at least sixty, maybe eighty people here, and although the guest of honor had not yet arrived it was clear that most of the younger ones were more determined to sink as much free booze as possible than to meet an alien face to face, even though that was the excuse they had advanced when insisting on being invited.

The whole shindig had caused grave alarm among

the security services, already dismayed by the inescapable necessity of preparing to introduce Landini to the President, to his colleagues the human astronauts, and then to the UN. It was all very fine and large for Landini to dismiss the fate in store for him with a wave, asserting again that because there were aleph-null of him it didn't matter. Being turned into a sort of zoological specimen *cum* exiled prisoner for the rest of his life was not a prospect to tempt Justin.

Who answered Chester now by saying, "You're right—it is the end of the world, isn't it? And what horrifies me is the petty scale it's all happening on."

"Petty?" Chester retorted, giving him a sharp glance. "I wouldn't say so! As complete a revolution in our world-view as we owed to Copernicus, or Einstein, and—"

Justin interrupted. "I'd call those petty, too! Most of what we regard as dramatic events took place at scientific congresses or in university lecture-halls. Now and then someone lost his temper; now and then there was a student rising to sack some particular stick-in-the-mud. But it was all small and slow by the standards of the rest of the world. What should have been attended by comets and volcanoes and signs in the heavens actually filtered through to the public consciousness over generations, like water seeping into a dry sponge. As late as the mid-nineteenth century Augustus de Morgan met someone who still believed in the four elements of the ancient Greeks."

"In that sense I can't disagree," Chester sighed. Catching sight of Herman a few meters distant, he waved, and the doctor excused himself to his former partner and approached.

"Glad to see you, Justin!" he exclaimed. "There's something I'd like to find out from you and Cinnamon before the star of the evening turns up . . . Where is Cinnamon?" He glanced around. "Is she not here?"

"I hope she'll get here later. Right now, she's in a hell of a state. *You* know why!"

"You mean she's taking seriously what she said this morning—I mean, what Landini says about insanity?"

"What's all this?" Chester demanded. Justin rapidly filled in the picture for him.

"And the hell of it is," he concluded, "so far Landini has been right. Everything he's told us was either most likely or next to most is happening! It seems he's just young enough to have gone through the first course of education in his world which took for granted the existence and effects of the poster, and he was taught the various scenarios which had been learned about from their aliens. Few of them, of course, as alien as we are by his standards; most were just people of his type from a variant branch of reality . . . It's no fun, believe me, having to accept that I was beaten to my one real piece of brilliance by literally an uncountable number of other people, many of whom I might not recognize as people."

Herman was a step behind. He said, "You mean he's predicting the future?"

"Not at all! You'll have to ask Edna if you want a really detailed analysis, but as nearly as I can understand his argument, it goes this way." A waiter passed with a tray of drinks; Justin exchanged his empty glass for a full one, and continued.

"The total dimensionality of the universe is of the order of aleph-four and may well be as high as aleph-five—in other words, much more infinite than infinity. Don't ask me for a quick course in Cantorian transfinites, please! You can find out about them from any good encyclopedia, or computer terminal.

"But you can discard at least one and maybe two orders of universes because they aren't being perceived by anything we would call perception.

"You can discard another order because so far as

we can tell nobody in them is liable to hit on the poster principle.

"We are still stuck with at least as many universes in which people—using the term in its broadest sense—do invent it, as there are possible curves in our universe: that is, more than there are points on a line, or in a solid volume, and more than the count of all conceivable numbers both rational and irrational."

By this time he was at the center of an enlarging group of fascinated listeners, including the fair young man from the supermarket, who had a pretty woman a few years older by his side.

"The greater the distance over which you operate a poster, the less your original resembles what arrives at the receiver. As I told you this morning, we've learned that the purpose of his people's space program is to launch more and more posters into the interstellar void, so as to establish contact with more and more alien intelligences."

"My God," said Herman softly. "This make our Project Ear seem like the bumblings of a Stone Age tribe!"

"Precisely!" Justin snapped. And could not help remembering the crash of those beautifully-shaped girders as the radio-telescope array was demolished . . . He overcame his pang of unreasonable sorrow.

"But what about volunteers?" Chester pressed.

"They have no shortage. He calls them pilgrims. It's one version of the contact scenario he was taught about, but not the only one. People decide they would like to sacrifice themselves so that others may benefit from direct contact with non-human creatures. So far they have very few; he says they expect to do better when they develop a hibernation technique so that posters can be operated nearer to other solar systems."

"Does there have to be a living person in the poster when it operates?" inquired the fair young man.

"Obviously. Otherwise all you'd get would be a

sample of interstellar dust, or whatever. But I don't think that's quite what Herman wanted to ask about."

Sipping his drink, Herman shrugged.

"I'm still baffled by the fact that he speaks English!" he declared. "You'd think it necessarily followed that he must speak a different language, have different concepts, even if only because he's physically a different shape!"

"This is because the operation of a poster"—the statement came from Edna, who had also joined the group and, with Levi trailing her, was working her way closer to Justin—"the operation of a poster is equivalent to a crisis-point in catastrophe theory. You could think of the cultures which have developed the poster as being like parallel ridges of a particular degree of probability, with slopes of lesser probability on either side. Transfers take place between levels of equivalent probability; this is why when an injured human called Landini was posted from orbit a correspondingly injured alien called Landini turned up in his place. If there's a computer-screen handy I can show you a pretty neat sketch I worked out yesterday and put in store. By the way, where's Cinnamon? I want to congratulate her on the programs she wrote for the computers at Chester U. They've generated daemons which take this kind of argument for granted. I never worked with such powerful tools before." Her face was aglow with enthusiasm.

"So powerful," Justin said sourly, "they appear to be taking over from us."

There were blank looks from everyone except Edna, who gave a loud sigh.

"That seems to be the case," she agreed.

"What's that supposed to mean?" the fair young man demanded.

"The crucial form of perception which makes poster operation feasible is not human, or even organic, at least not in the cluster of realities that we and he belong to. We can only reason *about* transfinites. Computers of the kind we've developed during the past half-century are now capable of reasoning *with* them, and that's the only thing which has made posters possible."

"It's true," Justin muttered. "We can give a name to something like rho-space. We can make hypotheses and even deductions about it. But the machines we've created can handle it as a datum—"

"There's Cinnamon!" Levi cried, waving frantically. She had just entered, seeming shy as a teenager at her first grown-up party, dressed—as all of them were—in her ordinary working clothes. "Instant City" was as yet ill-equipped to furnish its citizens with luxury goods.

Smiling a little wanly at everyone who tried to delay her, she made her way to Justin's side and took his hand like a weary swimmer clutching the rail at the end of the pool.

"Have you seen what it's like outside?" she murmured in an uncharacteristically subdued tone.

"What do you mean?"

"The people who haven't been allowed in here are holding a meeting. They're shouting. General Lane has decided to post armed guards. He thinks they may try and break in by force."

"But everyone's been promised a chance to meet Landini—" Herman began.

"They know as well as you or I that some won't get it," she replied simply. "They're frightened of being on the spot at the greatest event in history, and having nothing to tell the folks back home."

Seizing a drink, she poured half of it down her throat at one go. And added, "He foretold this as well, you know."

"But according to what I heard," objected the fair young man, "he said he'd never seen people like us before!"

" 'Never saw' doesn't mean 'never heard of'," Cinnamon answered. "He's incredibly calm, but underneath he must be terrified of us. Not just of being stranded—of being here!"

"He seems to be pretty good at throwing a scare into other people," Herman said caustically. "I'm glad you're calmer than this morning. Surely if what you believe is true there are an infinite number of universes where you and Justin won't—ah—break down, like you were suggesting."

"I wish you hadn't mentioned that," Justin said after a pause in which he worked out what he had earlier missed. "I think it's an unwarrantable assumption."

"And what else has he been wrong about?" Cinnamon countered. "According to the scenarios he learned about in school the chance of people with our type head, our type brains, reacting rationally to the impact of intelligent non-humans is next to zero! The reason he never saw people like us before is because we are among the versions that go crazy and wreck everything rather than share the universe with other people!"

Her hand was now so tightly closed on Justin's, it was painful. He eased free, patting her shoulder.

"Here comes the star attraction," he murmured. "Now you'll have the chance to talk it over with him in company instead of on your own. Maybe it was jumping to conclusions."

"When they have to deliver him under armed guard?" she retorted. "Don't make me laugh . . . Or rather: please do! If you don't, I think I'll have to cry!"

NINETEEN

today feels like sunday
a late lazy breakfast
a stroll to the park
but the streets are so crowded
the stores are all open
oh my god it's monday after all

Landini had let his facial hair grow. Neatly trimmed, it almost concealed the difference in his mouth and jaw. In fact, apart from his curious stance—he walked with his torso leaning markedly forward—he was not unhandsome in his hastily-adapted garments. But it had turned out he was myopic, and it was odd to see him wearing the glasses that had been specially made for him.

Two men with the indefinable air of Secret Service operatives escorted him through the door and then melted into the background. Simultaneously Chester, striding towards him, launched a chorus of *For He's a Jolly Good Fellow*. He had a clear light baritone voice that carried well.

The gesture was ridiculous, but so absolutely right that within moments everybody had taken up the words. Conducting as he went, Chester made his way to Landini's side and called for three cheers, which were loudly delivered. On a nearby table were ranged glasses of champagne; seizing one, he then called for a toast.

"Here's to the people without whom our new friend would not be here—the inventors of the poster, Justin and Cinnamon!"

Helping himself to a drink, Landini gave the toast

132

along with the others, though with what Justin suspected of being a wry expression. There followed a rattle of applause and someone called out, "Speech!"

Someone was bound to, Justin sighed to himself. But he shook his head vigorously enough to escape the chore, and—much relieved—people crowded around Landini with a barrage of eager questions.

Chester stood by with a benevolent expression, rather as though the poster, as well as this party, had been his idea. Under her breath Cinnamon confided to Justin, "Since you told me what Chester was like in your old world, I've come to recognize a lot of what you described in this version of him, too. I don't like him any the less for it. It must be hell if you're born into that kind of predicament. When do you ever get the chance to do something that's entirely your own?"

Justin nodded, though his thoughts were elsewhere. "Want to get next to Landini?" he suggested.

"Not until the first enthusiasm dies down. Give it an hour—or leave it up to him, if he wants to talk to us. In any case I think we're about to be attacked ourselves."

She was right; a dozen or fifteen people, late in making for the alien, had decided to make do with second best and were heading this way.

For the first ninety minutes it went on looking as though Chester's idea had been an inspiration. Although he was drinking a great deal of champagne, Landini showed no sign of his ordeal, and—judging by the outbursts of laughter which ascended from his vicinity—he was able to crack jokes. Even the Secret Service agents relaxed and dared to smile.

But then, just as trays laden with food were being brought in—by volunteers, since "Instant City" as yet lacked such trimmings as robot waiters—an altercation broke out. Amazingly, it was Dr. Rotblat who raised her voice to an ill-tempered pitch.

"It simply isn't *believable!*" she declared.

What? Chatting with Herman, Levi and a small group of others, Justin—like most of those present—had been keeping one ear cocked in Landini's direction, and now broke off what he was saying.

"I know what she can't believe," Herman muttered. "That someone so different can speak English."

"She's not alone," Cinnamon answered softly. "But we've accepted the truth—why can't they?"

Thus far the disagreement had been conducted in reasonably polite terms. Now, however, Landini lost his temper.

"Of all the stinking luck for me to wind up among a bunch of third-rate clods like you!"

There was an abrupt, glacial silence. Finding herself at its focus, Elaine shrank back, looking nervously around her for support.

"I only tried to explain—"

"You made it perfectly clear!" Landini barked. "You're too damned thick between the ears to recognize plain facts when they come up and stare you in the face! Maybe if they kicked you in the ass you might react! Oh, *shit*—I've had enough of this rôle-playing! Where are Cinnamon and Justin? At least they talk a bit of sense occasionally!"

But as he made to stride away Chester caught his arm.

"Third-rate clods, did you say?" he murmured in a dangerously sleek voice.

"Oh, nothing personal, Chester," Landini sighed; he had displayed no difficulty in telling his acquaintances apart, despite their radically different features. "But put yourself in my place for a moment, will you? The reason I never saw people like you before is because every contact with your sort turned out to be abortive. I mean, in the world I come from. After posters have been in use a generation or two—and we didn't build a handful and try and keep 'em secret, remember! We built millions and we honored their inventor as one of history's greatest geniuses! Listening over there, are you?" This with a wave to Justin. By now he had the attention of the entire room.

"Yes, we built as many as we could because we were excited by what we'd discovered! We'd found the key to an inexhaustible range of new experiences, right? But because there are so many, you don't try and learn about them all; you compromise. You learn generalizations, and from each stems a better and a worse alternative, and then from each worse one a better and a worse, and—and so on. You have to pass exams on this. It's become part of general knowledge.

"And one thing that stuck in my mind long after I quit school was that there are some areas of probability where the main sequence goes worse—worse—worse—worse . . . and never better! I didn't believe it, not in my heart of hearts, until it started happening to me. I didn't believe there could be an English-speaking version of us so dim-witted they couldn't respond sanely to the raw truth. Oh, I mouthed the usual responses: 'everything is possible in an infinite universe, therefore even the impossible is possible'—all that shit! But it never hit me until I realized that *I,* Eduardo Alfonso Landini, *me in person,* would have to suffer the rest of my life among people like *you*"—he thrust a long bony forefinger at Elaine, and she flinched back as though he held a knife—"who are proud, goddammit, *proud* of being stupid and bigoted and ignorant and dumb! And scared. Jesus Christ, above all else, scared! Convinced like that crazy general and that crazy admiral I got to meet that the poster is the invasion-channel for the Russians and the Chinese and the Egyptians and the—the—the Zulus! Of course it is, in an infinite universe, but before you cross *that* wild a string of possibilities you have to send your posters parsecs away at least, maybe to the other side of the galaxy, and that makes centuries and by then you've grown out of that kind of childhood nightmare!"

"Now just a moment!" Chester rapped. "According to what you've been telling people—"

"Short postings are more likely to bring in others of your own kind?" Landini interrupted. "Sure! But in the scenarios we're talking about, where there are world wars and nuclear attacks and all like that, posters don't get built, or if they get built they don't get deployed! Theoretically there must be universes where someone finds a functioning poster on the front doorstep when he goes to pick up the morning mail, but there you're right up in the aleph-two zone, at least."

By now Elaine had gathered her courage. Mutinously confronting Landini, she said, "But you've been telling people your history is as much like ours as your language!"

"It figures. Why else should the machines swap me to one of your posters? The world-view has to be pretty consistent." Landini dabbed at the corners of his mouth with a paper napkin; abruptly his face took on its non-human characteristics again as they saw he was drooling like a slobber-chopped dog with the intensity of his emotion.

"Then was there a Hitler in the world you claim to have come from?"

Landini gave a slow, weary nod. "I guessed this was bound to come up. When I said our history was like yours, remember, I was still in a hospital bed. Over the past two or three days they've allowed me to read some relevant material, and that's why I just blew my top. This Adolf Hitler of yours: near as I can figure, he corresponds to a pan-German fanatic who acquired a small following during an economic depression but murdered his lover, a guy called Roehm, and spent the rest of his life in a lunatic asylum writing crazy letters to the government about Jewish money-lenders."

"What about Stalin?" someone demanded.

"He didn't change his name! As Iosip Dzhugashvili he did more than anyone to bring about reform in Russia!"

"The Viet-Nam war!" came another shout.

"You mean when the nationalists took over from the French colonial power?"

That produced a baffled silence for a second. Justin and Cinnamon had been working their way towards Landini; now they were within earshot of Chester, who had been forced a little away from him as everybody realized this discussion was crucial to the problem posed by the alien's arrival.

"Is what he's saying credible?" he muttered now.

"Absolutely," Justin replied, equally softly. "Remember that in my old world Landini worked on Project Ear."

"I was afraid you'd say something like that . . . My God! I was never glad before that I was born rich, but I am now!"

"Why?" Cinnamon hissed, moving close and taking his arm.

"Do you know what's been going on outside since the party started?"

They stared at one another. "What?" Justin whispered.

"The Secret Service men told me. One of the people who didn't get invited has leaked the whole story, and all hell is going to be let loose."

"But I thought they were going to take him to meet the President and then everything would be carefully planned so the public had a chance to adjust!"

"That was the intention," Chester sighed. "It got torpedoed. I guess we'd best try and turn the party off when Landini calms down, and then you and I and the rest of us who've kept our heads can have a conference and pick up the pieces. Oh, no!"—glancing back towards the focus of disagreement. "What's going wrong this time?"

Cinnamon checked him before he turned away. "Why did you say you're glad to be rich?" she insisted.

"Because if one of us didn't carry gigantic clout, things wouldn't merely be bad. They'd be intolerable. I'll explain later! Right now—"

The dispute surrounding Landini had just reached shouting pitch, but at the same moment there came a noise from outside, even louder, and abruptly the main door of the conference-room was flung wide. The Secret Service agents dived for cover, drawing pistols, while everyone else swung to stare at the intruders.

They were a dozen or so in number, led by a young man who was obviously very drunk. Wielding an iron bar like a club, he shouted, "Where's this phony alien, then? I want to tear the mask off him!"

Cinnamon's hand closed convulsively on Justin's.

Rising slowly to his feet, gun levelled, one of the Secret Service men said, "Drop your weapon. You're under arrest."

But he was cut short by Landini. Striding forward, taking station next to the man with the iron bar, he shouted, "Go ahead, then! Shoot, and make sure you hit me! I'd be better off dead than living among crazy murderous animals like you!"

And then, and only then, two of the newcomers emerged into the full light and revealed that they were carrying a miniaturized TV camera and sound-transmitter.

"Gotcha!" one of them said with deep satisfaction. "Care to pay us a few more compliments, Mister Man From Mars?"

TWENTY

you thought you were making
a pretty good impression
you felt you were liked
by the people you worked with
but one day abruptly
they said we're letting you go

It was dark at mid-morning in Cinnamon's apartment where she and Justin were hiding out on police advice; it was sufficiently high not to be overlooked, but—also on police advice—they had been told to keep the curtains closed. Just conceivably an assassin might strike from a helicopter.

But if he were to try that, he would as likely use a bomb as a gun. It made no sense. Justin had said so over and over, without effect. The world no longer made sense. Therefore, stirring little save to eat or drink or void what they had taken, infinitely too miserable to think of making love, they watched the planet's slide over the precipice into collective insanity as it was documented on television.

On one channel a sober, grave announcer stated that plans to introduce alien-Landini to the president had been cancelled owing to receipt in Washington of more than two hundred identical letters, each threatening to infiltrate people into the White House with dynamite sticks strapped under their clothes.

On the next, a comedian was sweating through a sketch based on the news, where each time he opened a door or closet a different monster appeared and called him momma.

Another: a Jesuit was confronting Edna, who had become *de facto* spokesperson for the philosophers of the world, and putting inane questions about Landini's claim to be a Catholic, mostly concerned with the Incarnation.

Yet another: someone who boasted of helping to found "Instant City"—but if that were true, had probably been hired as a cleaner for the brief period before the right machines for the job were delivered—was learnedly pontificating about news from Russia, where a group of professors had declared in *Izvestia* that no alien being could possibly speak a terrestrial language. He agreed, and maintained that Landini was therefore a hoax.

As for Landini himself, they knew he was in custody "for his own protection" somewhere in Texas still. The most skilful interrogation of Cinnamon's home computer terminal had failed to show them a means of finding out exactly where.

A fifth channel: a fundamentalist preacher was declaring with enormous fervor that Landini must be a devil, because the only intelligent beings the Lord ever created were Adam and Eve, and they were white, and their original sin was to engage in relations with their own children in order to propagate the species, and that was why the Lord made some of their children black, and if anything that stood up on its hind legs and talked to you wasn't precisely like Adam and Eve that was a sure sign that creature was accursed and the blessing of the Lord would rest upon anyone who got it, and the Godless servants of Satan who were trying to foist it on an unenlightened public, in the sights of a rifle and had it skinned and mounted and presented it to a church or a museum where the faithful for ever after might inspect this work of the Evil One . . .

"Oh my God," Cinnamon whispered when she had

watched long enough. "Ed's right. We are crazy. All of us!"

Justin hit the channel-change again. This time it was the local station at Chester, reporting that a mob had tried to break into the university and burn the Wright & Williams building.

Justin thought bitterly of the crowd he had seen on that day—so long ago, so (?) far away—when he arrived to find one of Chester's emissaries in the reception zone, and heard the news about Gunther's death. Once again it was Monday . . . but he was in another world, which he had imagined to be satisfactorily different from his old one, whereas in fact it was proving to be much too like it. A veneer had been penetrated; a skin had been peeled away; a bubble had been burst.

"But there must be *somewhere* a world where humans like us turn out to be sane!"

He hadn't realized until Cinnamon uttered that anguished cry that he had been voicing his miserable convictions. Now he responded as she caught hold of his hand, and marshalled his thoughts as best he could to answer her.

"You're invoking Landini's credo, are you?" he said at length. " 'In an infinite universe . . .' "

"Of course I am! If we've learned one thing from his arrival among us, it's that personal choice—free will—counts for much more than *I* ever imagined!"

"Our choice? Or the choice made by our machines?"

"They don't make judgments when they select the correspondence between posters! It's determinate!"

"The machines didn't choose to get themselves built!"

"Humans didn't choose to get themselves evolved!"

For a long moment they stared at each other, while the TV—switched to yet another channel, the last before they would have to start over—said something about an announcement from Japan that a computer team analyzing the rho-space concept expected to convert it into hardware within months.

At last Justin said, "There was an infinitely good chance that we could have got someone else."

She nodded. "Right! We could have got what he calls a pilgrim, willing to co-operate in his new setting. It's just bad luck we got a neurotic who'd rather die than live out his life among strangers—and who's too scared of suicide to take that way out of our world!"

Justin said slowly, "Suppose you or I had been pitched into a world as alien to us as ours is to his: would you or I have reacted as he did?"

"Finally you got my point!" she crowed, and flung her arms around him. "There must be an infinite chance, too, that our kind of human *can* turn out well—regardless of Landini's contempt for us!"

"Then there's an infinitely good chance of tuning a poster so that it never . . . No. It's useless. I can't think in infinite terms."

"There was a time when humans couldn't have conceived of transfinites. There was a time when we didn't calculate with infinitesimals; then they became the small change of high-school mathematics classes. For pity's sake, Justin, how can I make you believe you're a twenty-four carat genius facing the consequences of transforming the world?"

Giddy, clutching at her for stability in this fluid version of reality, he muttered, "I'd give anything not to be!"

The TV screen blanked. When it re-lit, it showed Chester on the doorstep of the building, with two companions, and the police guard who warily risked pressing the door-bell for them.

"Let him in," Justin sighed. "I'd rather have news from him than a machine. Ever since Gunther's death, machines have been making me feel insignificant."

The Chester who entered was shockingly more like the one Justin recalled from his other world than the one he had grown friendly with in this one. Stern-faced, formally dressed, he gruffly presented his companions: a lawyer named Funck, and a professional lobbyist from Washington, Maconochie.

Having brushed Cinnamon's cheek with his lips, and shaken Justin's hand perfunctorily, he dropped on the long seat and came to the quick of the ulcer.

"There's going to be a Senate sub-committee hearing. And you two are going to be crucified at it."

"What?" Cinnamon exploded.

"I'm afraid Mr. Chester is quite right," Maconochie said. He had a full rich voice, like an operatic baritone off duty. "Would you care to drop this in your player?"

He proffered a videotape. Cinnamon numbly complied.

At once a familiar face appeared, a man of late middle age being interviewed at a press conference. Both Cinnamon and Justin recognized him as the most reactionary of the Southern senators, but with great seniority. And they heard him say, "Why, the first thing we have to establish is who stood to gain what by perpetrating this disgusting hoax on the good sense of the folk of our great nation. I do hear tell that upwards of several billion dollars—"

Cinnamon cut the sound with a violent gesture. *"He's* going to chair the committee?" she rasped.

"I'm afraid so," Funck agreed.

"Then I'm done for, at least." Cinnamon slumped on the seating. "He never believed a black could invent anything better than a cocktail mix."

The tape was spooling on. More faces were appearing. None gave any reassurance. There was nobody among them who understood—so Funck stated—even the principle of scientific method.

"We're running scared," Chester said meditatively, cancelling the tape and accidentally bringing back a TV channel, chosen at random. It showed hazy, hand-held-camera shots of a riot in a small town in the Mid-West. Cinnamon restored the sound. They caught a fraction of the commentary: because of a rumor that the alien had been taken from Texas to this former Army town in Kansas, the hospital had been stormed and set on fire.

"And all this is my fault!" Justin said, not wanting to but having to, feeling the weight of responsibility of all his aleph-null counterparts as though it were the dead weight of a lifetime's sin.

"What?" Chester glanced round. Then, unexpectedly, he began to laugh.

"What the hell is supposed to be funny?" Justin barked.

"Oh, man . . . !" Suddenly Chester was relaxed again, and the smart suit he wore seemed subtly wrong. "You didn't get it yet? Now I truly do believe you are from other worlds, you and Cinnamon both. Listen, friends, and pay considerable heed!"

He hunched forward, eyes sparkling, transformed on the instant into a seeming synthesis of the best Justin remembered from both versions of him: the human warmth on one hand, the authoritative command on the other.

"You hit me, Justin, with reference to Zena di Cassio—hmm? Anyone who had researched my background that thoroughly must have done a near-to-perfect job. But you never mentioned then or since another thing I was expecting to hear from you about. And as soon as I realized that, it dawned on me that Cinnamon hadn't mentioned it either. Not since she got posted. Not since you got posted.

"And since I'd sunk my appropriation for pure research for eight mortal years into it—a clear eight million dollars after tax—I figured I might be well advised to keep my mouth shut. That's why you never met Joe Funck before. If you had done, you would have." Triumphant, he sat back.

"I don't understand," Justin said after a pause, and glanced at Cinnamon, who shook her head.

With a grin that reminded Justin of the other Chester talking about confidence tricksters, the millionaire resumed.

"For a while, I swear I suspected you of being ringers. I thought of some grandiose scheme to persuade me that being posted gave access to—oh, tomorrow's news, maybe, by a faster-than-light route, or psychic data acquired in rho-space during transit. You must admit, the whole poster concept is so outlandish, everybody out there"—with a wave towards the windows—"is still struggling and will be for generations.

"But what's convinced me that you are what you claim to be . . ." He gave a wry, self-deprecating grin. "Since being posted, neither of you has asked me about the research project we set up to establish what happens when you operate a poster without knowing there's a receiver tuned to it.

"At first I thought that must be because you suspected all the places you went with me might be bugged. Bit by bit I decided that was wrong. You honestly didn't know—you honestly don't know even as of this moment—that I am in sole possession of the only two functioning posters on the planet which are not under direct government control."

There was a dazed silence. Eventually Cinnamon was able to whisper, "Well—what does happen?"

"Over this weekend we've finally figured out the right way to tackle that question . . . or our machines did. What it boils down to is that we don't have to put up with neurotics like Landini. We can get us pilgrims, eager to help."

"You came to the same conclusion as we did about Landini," Justin said.

"If he really did correspond to the person we'd known before, it was inescapable. Orphaned young, raised in a Catholic orphanage, lapsed from his faith, no close friends or emotional ties . . . I dug around some. Learned that his drinking problem nearly got him kicked off the Polly team."

"But the Landini I remember who worked on Project Ear," Justin muttered, "had plenty of friends, and drank socially but didn't have a problem, and . . . But that's not important. What is important is this." He drew a deep breath.

"Even if we can believe what Landini says about pilgrims—and 'in an infinite universe', and all that crap —won't we have to trade the kind of people we can least afford to lose in order to get them? Won't we have to spend our best?" He clenched his fists. "Why, it could become worse than a war, when you think how many helpers this sick species needs!"

Chester shook his head. "You're only half right. We must accept the impartial judgment of our machines, naturally. But remember this: the better the people we send, the better those we shall get back. On this sort of deal one cannot lose."

"How do you know?" Cinnamon demanded.

"Pack a bag and come where you'll find out."

TWENTY-ONE

behind this door or that
there is a beauteous maiden
behind that door or this
there is a half-starved tiger
let justice be done
although the heavens fall

"At first, of course," Chester admitted, "I had no idea what to look for. Nor did any of the people I was able to recruit. Bright enough, I promise you, but—well, what competent researcher, once established in a career leading to tenure, would look at a hare-brained proposition like mine? And I was damned well determined that, having come up with the project in the first place, having had probably the only original idea of my life, I wasn't going back to you on hands and knees to ask advice!

"So when we finally got it under way, I guess I wasted a lot of time and a lot of energy in random trials. Sometimes what we put in just disappeared; we got back dust. Sometimes we got back something indistinguishable from what we sent. Mostly we got back something recognizable but deformed. I felt kind of hurt when, after she was posted, Cinnamon stopped asking for her regular progress report—"

"But Justin knew!" Cinnamon burst out. "He . . ." Her voice trailed away. "Oh. No. The other Justin. But it's funny anyway, that he never mentioned it while we were together."

"I want to hear why you think we can get pilgrims!" Justin rapped, disregarding Cinnamon.

Chester chuckled. They were aboard a hired executive jet, and circling towards a landing at an isolated rural field. He seemed more and more at home in the sort of setting which would have suited his counterpart in Justin's former reality.

"It didn't dawn on me until after I learned about Landini, and not even then, not right away. I sidetracked myself. I said, 'What we ought to be sending out is requests for information about other worlds!' What did we get back? That's right: requests for information about other worlds. In most of the cases you couldn't have told the difference with a microscope."

Justin was gaping. He said, "My God, that should have hit me as soon as I realized Landini really did speak English!"

"No, you shouldn't," Cinnamon corrected gleefully. "Though I'm damned sure I'd have done the same, being hung up like I was on the notion that you must have a receiver ready for the thing being posted. How many tests did you run, Chester honey—and how did you keep your people from talking? Never mind that! I believe anything now! Answer the first one."

"How many? Oh, you're only talking about a hundred tests in all. Funding on this project has been kind of limited, even though I've been siphoning off my pure research funds to it. The two posters cost a million each, you know—"

"A million?" Cinnamon echoed in horror. "We cut our costs to three-eighty thousand!"

"You didn't have to bribe so many government officials," Chester answered somberly. "That's not cheap

. . . I often wished, you know, that I understood computers properly. I imagine I could have found the data I needed much more easily by sneaking it out of some major data-base link."

"Why didn't I think of this?" Justin mourned quietly to himself. "An alleged genius, and I never wondered what would happen if you tried to tune to a poster in another world!"

"Forget it!" Cinnamon ordered briskly. "Someone did. And eventually realized that you had to send *information*—right?"

Chester shrugged. "Send questions, you get questions. Send data, you get data. There are an infinite number of universes in the same pickle as us. There are an infinite number which haven't realized the poster crosses universe boundaries. There are an infinite number where even if they do they get disastrous results. There are an infinite number—And so on. The hell with it! What you do is go ahead on the assumption that these infinities cancel out; I'm working in terms of level odds. The rest doesn't matter. There are countless worlds where you and I are having this same conversation, only we're riding a giant dragon and breathing chlorine. Those opposite numbers we aren't apt to meet, right? Not yet. But with luck, when we can send posters out to the far stars . . ." He spread his hands.

Justin felt a chill crawl down his back. He said, "You know what you've done? You've beaten Project Ear. You've established communication with alien beings!"

"Mm-hm," Chester agreed. "And what's more in perfect English. We're about ready to land. Half an hour and you can prove it for yourselves."

The laboratory was in an abandoned barn in a lonely area; nearby, huge crates stencilled with the names of farm-machinery makers hinted at how the equipment had been brought here unchallenged. Inside, it was remarkably like a giant breadboard mock-up of what they were used to at Wright & Williams Inc. Except—

"Only one poster?" Cinnamon rapped at Chester.

"The other is in Mexico right now," said a tall young woman, striding forward. "We haven't figured out the reason, but on the basis of our limited tests that angle seems to give the best correspondence so far. Excuse me, but you are Dr. Wright, aren't you? And Dr. Williams? I'm Donna Jimenez."

"But I know you!" Justin blurted. "You were seconded by the DoD to work with us about two years ago."

She looked blank, and Chester put his arm around Justin's shoulders, murmuring close to his ear, "Another world. In mine, she's been working for me since we set the project up."

"Angle?" Cinnamon said loudly. Donna caught her meaning at once.

"Yes, that's something we gathered had been overlooked at your place. You can put a—a sort of angle of desirability on what you get through a poster by transmission from where you are, like here, to where another poster is in this world, like Mexico for instance, and then re-firing the receptor with no receiver set for it. It seemed logical that there must be some element of voluntarism involved, because with inanimate objects you get so much duplication, while with humans you get a world-shift instantly on the macro scale—"

"You say all this with such authority!" Justin broke in. "On the basis of a mere hundred tests?"

Donna looked at him blankly. "Well, not just on that alone," she said after a pause. "On the extrapolations we have. We rely on the Wright & Williams tap into the computers at Chester U. They've mapped all the possible outcomes for us and selected the optima. Why else do you think we sent the other poster to Mexico?

We haven't had time to work out that complex a problem by ourselves, have we?"

Justin drew a very deep breath. He said, "Now let me get this straight. Your computers here have already worked out how best to get useful information from other realities?"

"I . . ." Donna looked puzzled, and glanced at Chester for advice. When none was forthcoming, she tried again. "But surely you of all people must know that the destination of a poster transmission is determinable within aleph-null factors in a universe of aleph-four dimensions? I mean, I can get solutions to aleph-two orders of error just by punching a few keys on that board over there!"

"They don't know, Donna," Chester said solemnly. "They're both strangers here. Just reassure them that what you said about choice is true."

"Choice—? Oh, yes. I got sidetracked when I started to talk about voluntarism, right? We narrowed down the factors involved so *damned* tight that all we had left over was—" She spread her hands. "Well! The way the person being transmitted viewed the reality around him. We were forced to conclude that the computers supervising the transfer from poster A to poster B were taking into account factors so subtle no human mind could comprehend them, because they *are* the human mind."

"You mean when selecting a receiver," Justin whispered, "the computers make associations so fine that even the very thoughts passing through one's head have to be counted?"

"Even? Above all!"

"But—but that implies you could control your trip!" Cinnamon cried. "Using hypnosis, maybe!"

"But if you've been posted yourself, you must know that," Donna said, looking more puzzled than ever, seeming to doubt whether these people before her could really be the inventors of the poster. Chester intervened.

"Both of you did. We checked this out on the computers, and it fits. Cinnamon wanted a world where her Justin loved her. Justin wanted a world where Cinnamon loved him. Both wanted one where resources were better used and there was more personal liberty. Here you are. If I risked going through a poster, where would I wind up? In a world where I was global dictator, more than likely! Thanks to the way I was brought up . . . But friends, friends!" He put his arms around them both. "The goal and aim of the pilgrims is to exchange their rôles across the realities in order to seek out the universe where each can do the most good to their fellow beings!"

There was a stunned silence. It was perhaps the grandest claim any of them had ever heard or dreamed of.

"What proof do you have?" said Cinnamon at last.

"No proof. There is an infinitely valid chance that what we have received through the poster is a trap laid by a complex of evil universes." Chester shrugged. "But there must be an infinitely good chance of the trap failing, remember. Come and look at the tablets of stone which have been handed us from on high. Or somewhere."

His false jocularity failed to disguise his awe. And a few minutes later Justin and Cinnamon were sharing it. Encyclopedias which looked deceptively like any other until they were opened, whereupon a different history emerged; pictures of cities with familiar names —New York, London, Paris, Moscow, Peking—which were unrecognizable; newspapers bearing dates far into the future, reporting events without terrestrial referents, many not printed on actual paper . . .

"The chairman of the Senate sub-committee," Cinnamon said, not glancing up, "is going to ask how much it cost you to perpetrate this elaborate hoax."

"I know," Chester sighed. "But . . . Well, let me show you the most astonishing thing we've ever received. We got it in exchange for a summary of our predicament which I typed out in despair. It's the first time we've ever had anything so totally different from the original."

He proffered a sheet of paper bearing a text in a plain conventional type-style, as though it had come off any of the printers here, or at Chester U, or anywhere. It read:

For all those Earths where the inventors of the poster were among the first to make a pilgrimage without a destination, we have a bias of aleph-one in favor of a desirable outcome. For those where they delayed, we have the inverse.

"But this means that someone out there . . ." Cinnamon's voice failed her.

"Must be as far ahead of us as we of animals, and concerned," Chester supplied.

"Goodbye, crown of creation," Justin said humorously. "I have to accept that we've moved into a mode of reality where the universe is perceived more perfectly by our creations than by ourselves. I think we poor mobile creatures of instinct and heredity can only vaguely suspect what happens in the richer world of our successors. We're like the mobile spawn of barnacles or seasquirts, incredulous before the sessile preferences of our elders. Goodbye starships, goodbye colonies in space and the conquest of other planets . . ."

"I'm content with that," Chester said. "I guess I'm an axolotl—a juvenile form which will never grow up. But someone obviously has to. I guess there was a *first* creature to breed on land, a *first* creature to mate on the wing, a *first* creature to reason instead of react . . . These machines which you've devised have given us a degree of liberty we could never otherwise have conceived.

"What are you going to do about it?"

They stood there for a long, long while, listening to the clash and thunder of more universes than anything so petty as a human being was equipped to count. And then . . .

Exciting Space Adventure from DEL REY